主位推进模式视角下的
汉语散文英译研究

Translation Studies of Chinese Prose from the
Perspective of Thematic Progression Patterns

李 健 著

吉林大学出版社
·长春·

图书在版编目(CIP)数据

主位推进模式视角下的汉语散文英译研究 = Translation Studies of Chinese Prose from the Perspective of Thematic Progression Patterns / 李健著. — 长春：吉林大学出版社，2022.12
ISBN 978-7-5768-1347-0

Ⅰ.①主… Ⅱ.①李… Ⅲ.①汉语－散文－英语－翻译－研究 Ⅳ.①I207.6 ②H315.9

中国版本图书馆CIP数据核字(2022)第245757号

书　　名：主位推进模式视角下的汉语散文英译研究
Translation Studies of Chinese Prose from the Perspective of Thematic Progression Patterns

作　　者：李　健著
策划编辑：邵宇彤
责任编辑：杨　平
责任校对：王寒冰
装帧设计：优盛文化
出版发行：吉林大学出版社
社　　址：长春市人民大街4059号
邮政编码：130021
发行电话：0431-89580028/29/21
网　　址：http://www.jlup.com.cn
电子邮箱：jldxcbs@sina.com
印　　刷：三河市华晨印务有限公司
成品尺寸：170mm×240mm　　16开
印　　张：10
字　　数：168千字
版　　次：2023年1月第1版
印　　次：2023年1月第1次
书　　号：ISBN 978-7-5768-1347-0
定　　价：58.00元

版权所有　　翻印必究

Abstract of the Book

With the rise of text linguistics and its application to translation studies, text is gradually becoming the focus in the theory and practice of translation both at home and abroad. Approaching translation from the angle of text entails an adequate consideration of textual cohesion and coherence. Thematic Progression (TP) and the resultant TP patterns reflect the macro structure of a text and act as an important means to achieve cohesion and coherence of a text, so they serve as an important reference in a translator's decoding the Source Text (ST) and encoding the Target Text (TT). After a survey of studies on theme, thematic structure, thematic progression and TP patterns, as well as applications of these theme-based theories to text-oriented translation studies, we have found that explorations in this field up to the present are characterized by theoretical speculations supported by some illustrative examples and that empirical study is badly needed, so the present research, under the guidance of Descriptive Translation Studies (DTS), intends to describe the transference of TP patterns in Chinese-English textual translation on the basis of our observations of existing translated texts, summarize the laws of transference, and then probe into the conditioning factors underlying the transference. Both qualitative and quantitative approaches are adopted in our research.

Based on analyses of our selected materials in line with the notion of "thematic progression" defined by Danes, 14 kinds of TP patterns are discovered and the respective distribution frequency of all these kinds of TP patterns in the original texts and translated texts are also offered. Through paragraph-based observations, it is found that three different strategies are adopted by the translator in dealing with TP patterns of the original texts. Through sentence group-based observations, it is discovered that the occurrences of unchanged TP patterns are relatively fewer than those of changed TP patterns in the total transference of TP patterns, and that ten types of transference of TP patterns occur with much higher frequency, which represent to a considerable degree the laws of transference of TP patterns in Chinese-English textual translation. Thematic changes are found to be directly responsible for the changes of TP patterns in textual translation. The conditioning factors underlying the transference of TP patterns include linguistic and cultural factors, and the translator's purpose in conducting specific translation activity.

内容提要

随着语篇语言学逐渐兴起并广泛地应用于翻译研究,语篇逐渐成了国内外翻译理论研究和翻译实践的关注点。从语篇视角研究翻译必须体现出语篇的衔接性和连贯性,而主位推进模式体现出了语篇的宏观组织结构,是保证语篇衔接性与连贯性的重要手段,也是译者解读源语语篇和构建译语语篇时的重要参照。本书简要回顾了有关主位、主位结构、主位推进和主位推进模式的研究成果,以及这些主位相关理论在语篇翻译研究中的应用,发现目前的相关探讨多为理论上的思辨,辅以少量例证,而缺少实证性的研究。本书在描写译学的总体框架下细致观察具体的翻译文本,并在此基础上描述现代汉语散文语篇英译过程中主位推进模式的转换,总结其转换规律,进而分析其深层次的制约因素,研究过程中采用了定性研究和定量研究相结合的方法。

根据Danes所定义的"主位推进"概念,本书在对所选取语料进行分析的基础上,共发现了十四种基本的主位推进模式,并分别统计出了这些主位推进模式在源语语篇和译语语篇中的分布情况。然后,以段落为单位进行观察,发现译者针对原文中的主位推进模式有三种不同的转换策略;以句群为观察单位具体分析翻译过程中主位推进模式的转换情况,发现不变的比率略低于改变的比率,而且主位推进模式改变时出现了频率较高的十种情形,它们应该在很大程度上代表了现代汉语散文语

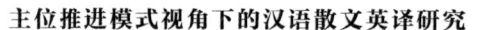

篇英译过程中主位推进模式的转换规律。研究表明，导致主位推进模式改变的直接原因是主位的改变，其转换的深层次制约因素包括语言和文化层面上的制约因素，以及译者的翻译目的。

Contents

Chapter 1　Introduction　　　　　　　　　　　　　　　　　　001

　　1.1 The Theoretical and Practical Value of the Research　　　003
　　1.2 Relevant Research at Home and Abroad　　　　　　　　004
　　1.3 Goals of the Research　　　　　　　　　　　　　　　　008
　　1.4 Focus of the Research　　　　　　　　　　　　　　　　011
　　1.5 Research Methods　　　　　　　　　　　　　　　　　　012
　　1.6 Innovations of the Research　　　　　　　　　　　　　014
　　1.7 Structure of the Book　　　　　　　　　　　　　　　　015

Chapter 2　Literature Review　　　　　　　　　　　　　　　017

　　2.1 Researches on Theme-Based Theories　　　　　　　　　021
　　2.2 Researches on Applications of Theme-Based Theories to Textual
　　　　Translation Studies　　　　　　　　　　　　　　　　　023

Chapter 3　Thematic Progression and Literary Text Analysis　035

　　3.1 Common Patterns of Thematic Progression　　　　　　　038
　　3.2 Application of TP Patterns in Literary Text Analysis　　042

Chapter 4　Thematic Progression and Textual Translation　　051

　　4.1 Descriptive Approach to Translation Studies　　　　　　053
　　4.2 Patterns of Thematic Progression in Texts　　　　　　　055
　　4.3 Thematic Progression in Textual Translation　　　　　　060

I

Chapter 5   Research Design   073

   5.1 Research Questions   075
   5.2 Research Hypotheses   076
   5.3 Data Collection   077
   5.4 Research Methods   078
   5.5 Research Feasibility   079

Chapter 6   Transference of Patterns of Thematic Progression in Textual Translation   081

   6.1 Data Processing   083
   6.2 Strategies of Transference of TP Patterns (Based on Paragraph)   100
   6.3 Transference of TP Patterns (Based on Sentence Group)   104
   6.4 Analysis of the Changes of TP Patterns   112

Chapter 7   Factors Underlying the Transference of TP Patterns in Textual Translation   123

   7.1 Linguistic Factors   126
   7.2 Different Thinking Patterns Between Chinese and English   130
   7.3 Translator's Purposes   134

Chapter 8   Suggestions for Future Research   139

   8.1 Findings of the Present Research   141
   8.2 Limitations of the Present Research   142
   8.3 Suggestions for Further Research   142

References   144

Appendix   150

Chapter 1

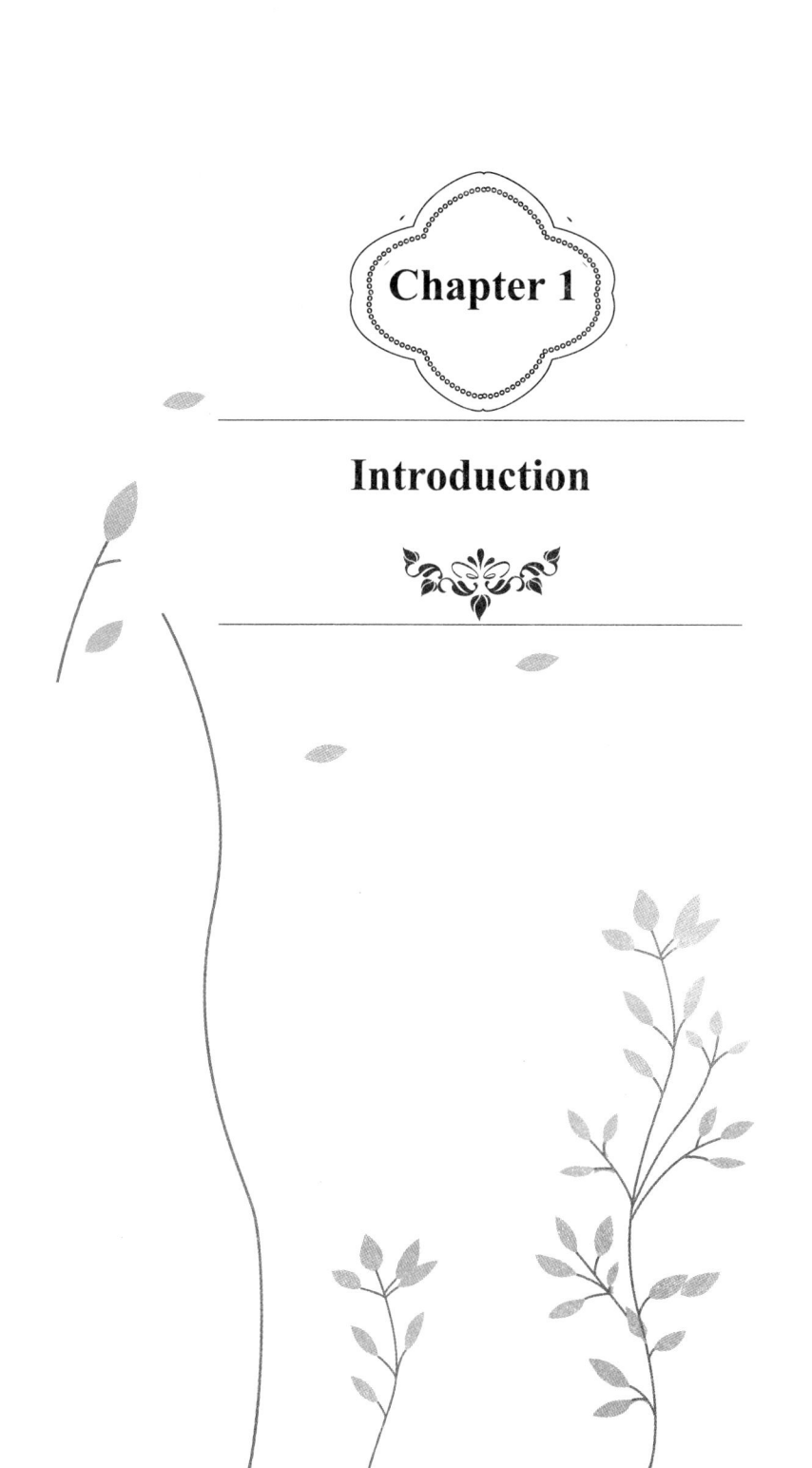

Introduction

English translation of Chinese modern literary works plays an important role in spreading Chinese culture to the whole world, which is of great significance in telling Chinese stories overseas, constructing the national image of China as well as the cultural identity of the Chinese nation, and promoting dialogue and communication between different civilizations. Therefore, the research on English translation of modern Chinese literary works has both academic significance and practical value. In this research field, the study on English translation of modern Chinese prose is a hotspot for translation studies in recent years.

1.1 The Theoretical and Practical Value of the Research

In the first place, this research can enrich the interdisciplinary research on English translation of Chinese prose. Under the framework of Descriptive Translation Studies (DTS), this research is approached from the angle of the transformation of TP patterns(patterns of thematic progression) in textual translation. By doing so, this research describes the transformation strategies in the process of English translation of modern Chinese prose, summarizes the laws of transformation, and probes into the motivations and underlying mechanism of the transformation, so as to provide a different research paradigm and theoretical reference for future studies on English translation of modern Chinese prose.

In the second place, this research can enhance the scientific accuracy of studies concerning English translation of Chinese prose. Empirical research based on a large-scale translation corpus, as this research does, can not only improve the scientific nature and verifiability of translation studies with regard to Chinese prose, but also meet the inherent requirements and development trend of translation studies as an empirical discipline.

Apart from the theoretical significance mentioned above, this research can serve as a guide in the practice of translating modern Chinese prose into English. The laws of transformation summarized from this research can enable us to have a better understanding of the process of turning modern Chinese prose into English, deepen our cognition of English translation of modern Chinese prose, and thus play a guiding role for the translators' reference when they try to render modern Chinese prose into English.

Last but not least, this research can promote the spread of splendid Chinese culture to the rest of the world. The results of this research can help translators adopt reasonable translation strategies and choose effective translation methods, and thus improve their capacity of translating modern Chinese prose into English. By doing so, they can accelerate the global dissemination of excellent Chinese culture.

1.2 Relevant Research at Home and Abroad

1.2.1 Research on English Translation of Modern Chinese Prose

With the implementation of the "going global" strategy of Chinese culture, the research on English translation of Chinese modern literary works has attracted extensive attention in domestic academia in recent years, and has produced fruitful research results. However, most of the research in this field has focused on the English translation of modern Chinese novels. By contrast, the relevant research on English translation of modern Chinese prose is relatively insufficient, which is mainly reflected in the following three aspects.

Firstly, the research on English translation of modern Chinese prose has not yet attracted due attention among scholars. According to the search results collected from the website of CNKI, there are in total 482 journal papers and dissertations with the key words of "prose translation" or "English translation of prose", of which less than 10 papers have been published in CSSCI source journals. Compared with the research results of relevant literature on English translation of modern Chinese novels, the number is noticeably small.

Secondly, the current research is mainly concentrated on a few writers, such as Zhu Ziqing, and focuses on a small number of classic modern Chinese prose and their English versions, such as the essay *Moonlight in the Lotus Pond* written by Zhu Ziqing. Generally speaking, this kind of case studies is not sufficient for us to investigate the overall features and discover universal laws of translating modern Chinese prose into English.

Thirdly, the research perspective remains relatively narrow and there is still much room for future exploration. Most of the existing research results have probed into the English translation of modern Chinese prose from such perspectives as translation aesthetics, reception aesthetics, artistic image and special charm (Wang, 2006; Liu, 2007; Zhou, 2015; Yuan et al., 2021). These kinds of studies often rely heavily on the researchers' breadth of knowledge as well as individual perception of prose. Therefore, the research conclusions reached frequently vary from one scholar to another, and the corresponding research methodology needs to be improved. In recent years, there have been an increasing number of research results with innovations in methodology.

A good case in point is the corpus-based comparative study of translator's styles (Liu, 2020), which, with the help of information technology and the application of modern linguistic theory, has enhanced the methodological innovations of the relevant research and thus improved the scientific nature of the research conclusions.

Although the existing studies have deepened our understanding of English translation of modern Chinese prose, the perspectives of the current research still need to be broadened, and the translation strategies and underlying mechanisms of translating modern Chinese prose into English still need to be further summarized and discussed. On the basis of previous research results, we can resort to the theory of text analysis and corpus-based methodology to further explore the process of translating modern Chinese prose into English based on large-scale corpus of modern Chinese prose and their corresponding translated texts. In addition, considering the diversity of prose types, such as argumentative writings, narrative writings, expository writings, etc., the research based on large-scale translation corpus can help researchers to seek correlations between different patterns of thematic progression in the translation process and the types of modern Chinese prose, so that we can arrive at more reliable and convincing research conclusions.

1.2.2 Research on Textual Translation Based on Patterns of Thematic Progression

Patterns of thematic progression are the arrangement and layout of language materials in a text, which reflect the structural framework of the text as well as the author's writing methods and communicative intentions. They can not only help the author produce a text effectively, but also can help the translator interpret the text accurately. Therefore, they serve as an important factor that needs to be handled carefully in textual translation. Scholars at home and abroad have already achieved a large number of research results in the research fields concerning thematic progression, which are mainly reflected in the applications of TP patterns to both text analysis and foreign language teaching, especially teaching of English Writing (Li, 2003; Wang et al., 2004; Liu et al., 2014; Shi et al., 2018). The application of thematic progression theory to translation studies can be roughly divided into three categories:

The first kind of research is the attempt of treating thematic structure as a translation unit (Baker, 2000; Fawcett, 2007; Liu et al., 2000; Li, 2002). According to the segmentation of theme and rheme in the clausal level and the features of translation practice, it is proposed by some scholars to analyze the source text and generate the target text with reference to thematic structure as the translation unit.

The second kind of research is the discussion of the functions of thematic progression in textual translation. Some scholars (Hatim, 2001; Zhao et al., 2003; Peng, 2016) argue that thematic progression can serve as a useful tool for translators to interpret and analyze the textual structure of the original text in the translation process, and that appropriate thematic progression can help the translators create a cohesive and coherent translated text.

The third kind of research is the exploration of the transference of TP patterns in textual translation. Some scholars (Hatim & Mason, 2001; Zhang, 2006; Liu, 2006; Li Jian et al., 2008) claim that the textual purpose and overall textual effect embodied by the patterns of thematic progression in the source text requires the translator to reproduce or reconstruct the similar patterns of thematic progression of the original text, in order to achieve the same or at least similar textual effect in the translation process.

Fruitful research results in the application of TP patterns to translation studies have been achieved so far, which has deepened our understanding of the translation process. However, the relevant research with regard to English translation of modern Chinese prose still remains not adequate and far from enough. What's more, most of the current research in this field relies heavily on the researcher's individual experience, that is to say, this kind of research is basically theoretical speculation supported by a small number of examples. By contrast, there is a lack of empirical research based on large-scale corpus, which is not conducive to observing and summarizing the universal laws of textual translation. Consequently, it is necessary to switch from the current prescriptive research to a descriptive approach, and, under the overall framework of Descriptive Translation Studies (DTS), make an in-depth and detailed description of the transference of TP patterns occurring in the process of English translation of modern Chinese prose. Based on an adequate observation, description and statistics of large-scale corpus, we intend to analyze the strategies involving the transference of TP patterns in the English translation of modern Chinese prose, summarize the laws of transference, and verify these laws in the practice of prose translation.

1.3 Goals of the Research

In this book we intend to apply the research methodology of descriptive translation studies to our research, and approach the English translation of modern Chinese prose from the perspective of the transference of TP patterns. Specifically speaking, we resort to large-scale translation corpus and comparative analysis of original texts and translated texts, in the hope of exploring the strategies and laws involving the transference of TP patterns in the process of translating modern Chinese prose into English, and expounding the underlying mechanism behind the transference of TP patterns.

Our first goal is to analyze the transference strategies and summarize the transference laws. We will make use of both qualitative and quantitative research methods to count up and then describe the transference of TP patterns in the process of rendering modern Chinese prose into English on the basis of large-scale translation corpus. The other goal is to explain the constraining factors and underlying mechanism behind the transference. We will investigate the constraints from different dimensions, trying to deepen our understanding of English translation of modern Chinese prose, broaden interdisciplinary paths to translation studies on modern Chinese prose, enrich translation theory and promote translation practice.

To be specific, the research involves the following four steps:

I Elaborating the functions of TP patterns in the English translation of modern Chinese prose

Patterns of thematic progression serve as an important formal device in producing a literary text, which often bear the author's communicative intentions and aesthetic preference. Therefore, it is necessary to illustrate the roles patterns of thematic progression play in the construction and interpretation of prose texts. Patterns of thematic progression also function as an important reference for a translator in the process of producing translations. Consequently, it is equally important to explain, the functions of TP patterns perform in text construction in the process of English translation of modern Chinese prose, and how the translator deals with the TP patterns of the original texts, and what impact different patterns will have on the overall textual effect of the target texts.

II Re-classifying the patterns of thematic progression in accordance with the Chinese prose texts and their English versions

According to our survey of the existing relevant literature, there have already been various theories on the classification of TP patterns, but it still seems insufficient for us to study prose texts. Therefore, it is of great necessity for us to observe and discover, according to the definition of TP patterns proposed by F. Danes, all the possible patterns of thematic progression occurring in both modern Chinese prose texts and their English translations and then re-classify the patterns of thematic progression based on large-scale corpus. Moving forward from this, we can also observe and describe the distribution features of TP patterns in the original Chinese texts and the translated English texts respectively.

III Analyzing the transference strategies of TP patterns in English translation of modern Chinese prose and summarizing the laws of transference

By making comparisons between the original Chinese texts and their English translations, we can count up all the transference of TP patterns in the process of translating modern Chinese prose into English, and then summarize the strategies of transference and extract the laws of transference on the basis of statistical data. Through the analysis of statistical data, we can give an analysis and description of the overall translational preference of translators in terms of the transference of TP patterns. Based on the previous steps, we can describe and analyze the translation strategies and methods adopted by the translators as far as the transference of TP patterns are concerned, and further analyze the translator's operational flexibility in dealing with the transference of TP patterns.

IV Explaining the causes and underlying mechanism concerning the transference of TP patterns in English translation of modern Chinese prose

Based on the statistical results and quantitative analysis of the transference of TP patterns in the process of translating modern Chinese prose into English, we will further probe into the motives and constraints of the transference made by the translators, including linguistic constraints (such as the paratactic characteristics of the Chinese language versus the hypotactic features of the English language), cultural constraints (such as different thinking patterns between the English people and the Chinese people), social and cultural background, the patronage (also termed as sponsors or initiators) of translation activities, translation purposes, the translator's subjectivity and some other constraints underlying the translator's transference of TP patterns.

1.4 Focus of the Research

The key points of the research are as follows:

Firstly, based on the previous classifications proposed by some scholars as well as our observations of collected corpus, we will re-classify the patterns of thematic progression occurring both in the original Chinese texts and in the corresponding translated English texts. How to carry out a reasonable and scientific classification and consequent statistical analysis, so as to ensure the scientific and reference value of the research conclusions, is a key point.

Secondly, to what extent have the translators preserved the original patterns of thematic progression in the Chinese prose and how have the translators changed the patterns of thematic progression if they cannot be preserved in the course of translation? It is essential for us to make a detailed observation, description and analysis of these transference and try to extract the transference strategies and regular patterns in this regard.

Thirdly, there must have been various causes accounting for the changes of TP patterns in the process of translating modern Chinese prose into English, hence the necessity to analyze the factors governing the translator's different choices and to construct the transference strategies and the underlying mechanism involving the transference of thematic progression in the English translation of modern Chinese prose.

There are some difficult points to be tackled in this research. On one hand, modern Chinese prose is copious and diverse. Therefore, when selecting corpus for our research, we should single out those excellent representative works of well-known writers and their corresponding high-quality English translations by first-class translators, so as to ensure the corpus from both languages is classical, typical and suitable for comparative studies. On the other hand, in order to accurately identify every pattern of thematic progression appearing in the source and target texts, we need to label the large-scale collected corpus, one by one, in strict line with its definition, and then to perform the statistics and classification, which entails a heavy workload and much difficulty in doing so.

1.5 Research Methods

In order to achieve our research goals, we will adopt the following research map: first, pin down the scope of research; second, collect the translation corpus for the sake of this research; third, label the Chinese original texts and the parallel English translations according to the definitions of theme and rheme; fourth, classify the patterns of thematic progression on the basis of the labeled texts; fifth, employ the guiding principles and research methods of Descriptive Translation Studies (DTS) to observe, describe and analyze the transference of TP patterns in the translation process; sixth, analyze the statistical results and summarize the laws of these transference; and the last step is to investigate both the restrictive factors and underlying mechanism in the course of prose translation.

According to the characteristics of this research, we adopt the following four research methods:

Descriptive research method: under the framework of descriptive translation studies put forward by G. Toury, we will give a detailed description of the transference strategies with regard to the patterns of thematic progression in the English translation of modern Chinese prose, extract the regular laws of such transference and finally explain the underlying mechanism.

Statistical analysis method: we will make an analysis of the statistical results of the transference of TP patterns in the translation process, on the basis of which we can discover the transference strategies and extract the transference laws, and then try to figure out the translators' preferences in making translational choices according to the statistical data.

Empirical research method: we will describe the distribution of TP patterns in the source and target texts and, on the basis of observing large-scale translation corpus, carry out statistics in terms of the transference occurring in the process of translating modern Chinese prose into English, and combine quantitative analysis with qualitative analysis in this research.

Comparative analysis of translation: as different levels of translation comparisons constitute the basis of translation studies, both the comparative analysis of original Chinese texts and their English translations and the comparative analysis of different versions of translated texts will be carried out, in the light of different research purposes.

1.6 Innovations of the Research

As a kind of basic theoretical research, the innovations of this research are reflected in the following two aspects.

Innovation of research methods: This research is done under the framework of descriptive translation studies, based on the observation, statistics and description of large-scale translation corpus. This kind of empirical translation studies help us switch from the traditional approach typical of theoretical speculations with a few supporting examples, widely used in previous relevant research, to a new approach intended for the research on English translation of modern Chinese prose. By doing so, we can also enrich the linguistics-based translation theory.

Innovation of research perspectives: Based on the statistical analysis of large-scale translation corpus, we will extract the regular laws concerning the transference of TP patterns in the process of translating modern Chinese prose into English, and probe into the underlying mechanism behind the transference. This kind of research focuses on the transference of linguistic forms and textual structure occurring in the English translation of modern Chinese prose, which is quite different from the previous research conducted from such angles as transference of semantic meanings and artistic images. By doing so, we can deepen the understanding of English translation of modern Chinese prose from a different perspective.

1.7 Structure of the Book

TP patterns are the important reference for translators to decode the Source Text (ST) and encode the Target Text (TT). The present research is designed, under the framework of Descriptive Translation Studies (DTS), to describe the transference of TP patterns actually happening in the process of Chinese-English textual translation on the basis of observing and analyzing the existing translated texts with comparison to their original texts, to summarize the laws of the transference, and to probe into the underlying factors for the transference. This research will enable us to deepen our understanding of textual translation and offer some guidance in our translation practice. Moreover, to probe into the laws of transference in translation through observing, describing and explaining the existing materials under the overall framework of Descriptive Translation Studies measures up to the requirements of translation studies as an empirical discipline.

The potential results of this research, with focus on the English translation of modern Chinese prose, can be used in the following fields. Firstly, as a basic research literature in the fields of English translation of Chinese prose as well as of text analysis, it can serve as a reference book for scholars in the research fields of translation studies and text analysis. Secondly, it can be used as a textbook for translation courses in colleges and universities, for the reference of teachers and students majoring in translation. Thirdly, it can also be used as a reference book for translators engaged in the English translation of modern Chinese prose in that it provides some useful translation strategies and practical methods to improve the overall effect of translation practice.

Chapter 1 gives a brief introduction of the present research. Chapter 2 reviews the relevant literature on theme, thematic progression, patterns of thematic progression as well as their applications to translation studies at home and abroad. Chapter 3 deals with the relationship between patterns of thematic progression and literary text analysis. Chapter 4 presents the theoretical framework for the whole research and discusses the application of TP patterns in textual translation. Chapter 5 puts forward the research methodology, including research questions, data collection, theoretical hypotheses and research feasibility. Chapter 6 offers the results of data processing, describes the transference of TP patterns by conducting statistical analyses of them, and then points out the causes for the various changes of TP patterns. Chapter 7 analyzes different factors underlying the transference of TP patterns in the translation process. Chapter 8 summarizes the main findings and the limitations of the present study, and also gives some suggestions for further research.

Chapter 2

Literature Review

With the rise of text linguistics, there appears a new trend of text-oriented translation theory, with its focus changing from the word and sentence to the text, and lots of researchers have been trying to establish a theoretical framework of translation based on text analysis. Applying theories of text analysis to translation studies includes both theoretical explorations and practical operations, where text has become the focus in the theory and practice of translation. Texture is regarded as one of the defining properties of being a text. Halliday (2000:334) holds that texture consists of the following textual components: thematic structure, information structure and cohesion. Thematic structure is one of the two structural features (the other being information structure) that create the texture of a piece of discourse or text. It is the structure of a clause which is divided into two parts: a Theme and a Rheme. Therefore, many scholars have discussed the application of Theme and thematic structure to the text-based translation studies.

Theme is put forward against the background of text as an important concept for describing the structure of a clause, and it is clause-based. However, it is the text, not just a single clause after another, that a translator confronts in the process of translating. If translation studies focus merely on the Theme and Rheme of the clause level, not on the progression of Themes and Rhemes in the process of clauses developing into a text, it is largely the same as treating clause or sentence as the unit of translation, which is not supposed to be workable in both the practice of textual translation and the text-oriented translation studies. The message conveyed in the clauses of a text is progressing constantly until a series of clauses developing into a paragraph and then a text, so approaching translation studies from the angle of text involves taking into consideration thematic / rhematic progression and the corresponding macro-structure of a text, because the notion of thematic/rhematic progression "has proved helpful in ridding basic theme-rheme analysis of its inherent sentence-orientedness" (Hatim, 2004:265) and finally displays the dynamic and coherent nature of a text.

To put it simply, Thematic Progression (TP) is the study of how Theme in a text is developed from clause to clause or larger stretches of text. TP plays an important role in maintaining coherence in text and it is closely related to the method of development in text. TP patterns are the forms of arranging the linguistic materials in a text, and they are the important means in fulfilling the textual functions, for they are of help not only to writers in producing their texts but also to translators in understanding the original texts. TP patterns display the framework and overall orientation of a text and reflect the author's methods and intentions of creating the text, so they are the factor deserving special consideration in textual translation. Explorations in applying TP patterns to text-based translation studies are currently focusing on theoretical speculations plus some typical examples and lacking in empirical studies, which is not favorable for us to observe and effectively describe the laws of transference in the process of translating.

In order to get a better understanding of the issue to be discussed in this book and carry out an in-depth study on the basis of the academic achievements of previous scholars in this field, we need to have a review of the research on theme-based theories as well as the research on the applications of theme-based theories to textual translation studies.

2.1 Researches on Theme-Based Theories

According to actual division of the sentence proposed by V. Mathesius, the founder of Prague School, every sentence can be divided from the viewpoint of its communicative functions into two semantic components: Theme and Rheme. The idea was later accepted and developed by M. A. K. Halliday, the master of Systemic Functional Linguistics. Studies on Theme and Rheme are generally focusing on the following respects.

2.1.1 Researches on Theme and Thematic Structure

Explorations on theme and thematic structure are centred on such aspects as those elements serving as the theme of a clause, markedness of the theme, the division of theme and rheme in a clause and the consequent thematic structure. Halliday (2000:37) and Thompson (2000:119) both hold that "as a message structure, a clause consists of a Theme accompanied by a Rheme". "The Theme is the element which serves as the point of departure of the message; it is that with which the clause is concerned." (Halliday, 2000:37) That is to say, the theme of a clause is simply the first constituent of the clause, and all the rest of the clause is simply called the rheme, the part in which the theme is developed.

Halliday (2000:42-48) discusses markedness of themes in English according to the choice of mood. Apart from that, Halliday (2000:334) identifies thematic structure as an important structural feature and one kind of structural cohesive devices of a piece of discourse or text. Fang et al.

(1995:20-24) apply the theory of theme and thematic structure from the Systemic Functional Linguistics to the studies on the Chinese language and probe into the thematic structure in Chinese texts. Zheng (2000:18-24) discusses, under the guidance of Halliday's theory of theme, the macro principles in the actual division of the sentence and some decisive factors in determining the theme of a clause in the Chinese language.

2.1.2 Contrastive Analysis of Thematic Structure in Chinese and English

According to the new linguistic typology advanced by American linguists Charles Li and Sandra Thompson (Li, 1976; Li & Thompson, 1981), English is a subject-prominent language whereas Chinese is a topic-prominent language. Baker (2000) argues that there tends to be a very high correlation between theme / rheme and subject/predicate in English. Li (2001) maintains that a clause in Chinese is essentially a semantic structure typical of "topic + comment". Wang (1999:15-19) analyzes and differentiates theme, subject and topic in English and Chinese based on the basic sentence patterns in the two languages.

2.1.3 Researches on Thematic Progression

The concept of "thematic progression" is initially put forward by Czech linguist F. Danes (1974:114). Studies on TP are concentrated on its relation to coherence in text. Li (1992:1-6), Zhang et al. (1994:27-33), and Yang (2004:7-10) all have discussed the relation between TP and textual coherence and hold that suitable TP helps to achieve coherence in text. Wang et al. (2004:48-52) examine TP and message parameters in text, and argue that message conveyed in the themes and connections between themes and their progression in a text should be understood in a specific semantic field.

2.1.4 Researches on Patterns of Thematic Progression

Scholars at home and abroad have summarized their respective kinds of TP patterns on the basis of their investigations on textual structure in English as well as other languages. Danes (1974:118-119) firstly put forward five common kinds of TP patterns, and from then up to the present, the frequently-mentioned classifications of TP patterns proposed in succession by researchers are as follows: four types put forward by Xu (1982:3-4); seven types by Huang (1985:34-35); six types by Huang (1988:81-85); three types by Hu (1994:144-145); and four types by Zhu (1995:7).

2.2 Researches on Applications of Theme-Based Theories to Textual Translation Studies

With the rise of text linguistics and its application to translation studies, text is gradually becoming the focus in the theory and practice of translation. Theme, as an important concept proposed under the background of text analysis to describe the structure of a clause, is widely used in the text-based translation studies. A review and summary of the relevant research of scholars at home and abroad in different periods can help us have a general understanding of this field and inspire new and in-depth thinking about this topic. Explorations in this field mainly focus on four aspects, i.e. theme as the unit of textual translation; transference of thematic structure in C-E & E-C translation; functions of thematic progression in textual translation; and transference of TP patterns in textual translation.

2.2.1 Researches on Theme as the Unit of Textual Translation

According to actual division of the sentence proposed by V. Mathesius, the founder of Prague School, every sentence can be divided, from the viewpoint of its communicative functions, into two semantic components: Theme and Rheme. The idea was later accepted and developed by M. A. K. Halliday, the master of Systemic Functional Linguistics. Halliday (2000:37) and Thompson (2000:119) both hold that "as a message structure, a clause consists of a Theme accompanied by a Rheme". "The Theme is the element which serves as the point of departure of the message; it is that with which the clause is concerned." (Halliday, 2000:37) All the rest of the clause is simply called the rheme, the part in which the theme is developed. Thematic structure, generally made up of a theme and and a rheme, is based on a clause. Halliday (2000:334) identifies thematic structure as an important structural feature and one kind of structural cohesive devices of a piece of discourse or text. Fang et al. (1995:20-24) apply the theory of theme and thematic structure from the Systemic Functional Linguistics to the studies on the Chinese language and probe into the thematic structure in Chinese texts.

The significance of studying theme and thematic structure is to understand the internal structure of clauses, the distribution of information in clauses, and its communicative functions. In fact, every text can be regarded as a sequence of themes, which is characterized by the mutual connections and progression of themes. The choice of theme means the starting point of information and development direction of a text. Thematic progression formed by theme and rheme reflects the structural framework of a text and effectively conveys the information of the text. The theme of a clause also plays a cohesive role, through the choice of which the author can guide the readers to make a coherent interpretation of the text.

Since the transference between two languages usually occurs at the level of clause in translation, theme plays an important role in the analysis, transference and construction of clauses in text-based translation and is of great significance to the cohesion and coherence of texts. Therefore, it is feasible to take theme as the unit of translation in the translating process. Through the known and new information contained in the theme and rheme, the translator can first understand the distribution of information as well as their role in the source text, on the basis of which he can then make linguistic transference. Moreover, in the process of constructing the target text, the choice of which component to act as the theme will affect not only the sentence structure in the target text but the cohesion and coherence of the text as well.

The initial attempt to introduce the theme-based theories into text-oriented translation studies is made by those researchers who take theme as the unit of textual translation. Xu (1982:8-9) firstly introduces theme and rheme into the field of translation studies, claiming that the theory of theme and rheme can help translators to understand the original text more accurately and guide their translation practice. Yang (1996:44-48) probes into the issue of semantic equivalence in English-Chinese translation from the perspective of theme and holds that the dislocation of themes in translation text will disrupt the information structure of the original text and affect the meaning transfer between the source text and the target text. Liu et al. (2000:61-66) suggest that the source text should be analyzed and transferred with theme / rheme as the unit of translation, arguing that this approach will be of direct help in the clause-constructing process, hence quite operable in the process of translation due to its own features and cohesive functions in the text.

What should be pointed out here is that taking theme / rheme as the unit of translation also demands our attention to the dynamic nature of information development in a text, otherwise it is equivalent to taking clause as the unit of translation. Since the information carried by clauses in a text is gradually developing till the clauses finally become a paragraph or even a whole text, the translation studies from the perspective of text analysis calls for our attention to thematic progression and the consequent macro-structure of the text. The translators should take into consideration the gradual progression of information and coherence of the text, rather than just operating at the level of theme and rheme.

2.2.2 Researches on Transference of Thematic Structure in Textual Translation

Since theme and thematic structure are of great significance for understanding the source text and constructing the target text, it is certainly desirable to maintain the thematic structure of the original text in English-Chinese textual translation. However, it is not always possible to copy the original thematic structure in the actual translation process, because both languages have their own distinctive characteristics in sentence structure. In this case, the translators should respect the unique features of different languages and make appropriate transference of thematic structure.

According to the new linguistic typology advanced by American linguists Charles Li and Sandra Thompson (Li, 1976; Li & Thompson, 1981), English is a subject-prominent language whereas Chinese is a topic-prominent language. Baker discovers that there tends to be a very high correlation between theme and subject in English by pointing out that "... there tends to be a very high correlation between theme / rheme and subject / predicate in the Hallidayan model. ... generally speaking, the distinction between theme and rheme is more or less identical to the traditional grammatical distinction between subject and predicate." (Baker, 2000:123) As a topic-prominent language, the Chinese usually does not have such an explicit formal cohesion as that in English. The sentences in Chinese are often organized together by means of parataxis, and there are a large number of sentences typical of "topic + comment" structure. Li (2001:200) claims that a clause in Chinese is essentially a semantic structure of "topic + comment" and basically the theme of a Chinese clause is its topic. Moreover, the theme of the Chinese language is not limited to the level of clauses, and sometimes there are both clause themes and sentence themes. This difference in thematic structure between English and Chinese is a factor that needs to be carefully handled in the process of English-Chinese textual translation. Applications of thematic structure to English-Chinese textual translation studies are mostly focusing on the relations between theme, subject and topic as well as their mutual transference in translation.

Baker (2000:141-144) claims that a translator cannot always be able to preserve thematic structure of the source text due to the differences in syntactic structure between different languages, and that what's important for the translator is to ensure that the target text has its own method of textual development and maintains coherence without disrupting the information structure of the source text. She probes in particular into the relations between theme in English and topic in Chinese, and discusses how to translate into English the "topic + comment" structure of the Chinese language. Fawcett (2007:85-90) argues that thematic structure can be well preserved in the transference between some languages, but cannot be preserved between some other languages, so a translator should not duplicate blindly thematic structure of the original text, instead, he needs to manipulate various means in the target language in order to achieve the same desirable textual effect. Ghadessy & Gao (2001:335-362) conduct research into the transference of thematic structure occurring in the translation process by comparing English texts with their Chinese versions through a quantitative approach for the first time.

Wang (1996:46-50) discusses in detail how to translate the topics of the Chinese clauses into English after a comparison of subject, topic and theme, arguing that the subject and word order of the sentences in the target text should be selected in line with the syntactic structure of English. Li (2002:19-22) applies the concept of theme to English-Chinese translation theory and describes the transference occurring in the themes of the clauses. In view of the differences in thematic structures between English and Chinese, he explores, on the basis of translation corpus, the mutual transference between subject themes in English and topic themes in Chinese, as well as the transference from implicit themes of Chinese clauses to explicit subject themes of English clauses. Yang (2003:84-88; 2006:23-28) discusses how to deal with theme and topic in English-Chinese translation as well as Chinese-English translation respectively on the theoretical premise that "English is a language typical of subject-predicate structure while Chinese is a topic-prominent language". He claims that in translating from English to Chinese, the translator should transfer the subjects of English clauses to the topics of Chinese clauses, and in translating from Chinese to English, the translator needs to transfer the topic-comment structure in Chinese to the subject-predicate sentence pattern in English, and make corresponding adjustments in terms of the themes and rhemes of the original text. Wang (2006:24-27) also explores how to handle the issue of theme in English-Chinese translation and maintains that in English-Chinese translation, the transference of theme and rheme structure between the two languages is largely equivalent to the proper transference of "subject + predicate" in English and "topic + comment" in Chinese. Cheng (2006:16-18) claims that one decisive factor affecting the quality of a translated text in Chinese-English translation is the correct choice of the subject, so she suggests that a translator should enhance his supra-clausal consciousness, take a sentence group or a paragraph as the unit of transference and make good use of thematic structure and thematic progression in the translating process.

These scholars mentioned above apply theme and thematic structure from the theory of text analysis to text-oriented translation studies, describe the phenomena of thematic transference occurring at the level of clauses in both English-Chinese and Chinese-English translation, and probe into the laws of transference of thematic structure on the basis of relevant translational materials. The conclusions reached so far, of course, need to be tested, modified and enriched on the basis of language data on a larger scale so that they can have stronger explanatory power to the translated texts and more powerful guidance to translation practice.

2.2.3 Researches on Functions of TP in Textual Translation

When a series of meaningful clauses develop into a piece of coherent text, the themes and rhemes of these clauses will inter-connect with each other and contribute to the flow of information in the text. The inter-connections between these themes and rhemes are termed as Thematic Progression (TP). The concept of "thematic progression" is initially put forward by Czech linguist F. Danes, who defines TP as "the choice and ordering of utterance themes, their mutual concatenation and hierarchy, as well as their relationship to hyper-themes of the superior text units (such as the paragraph, chapter …), to the whole text, and to the situation."(Danes, 1974:114) Thematic progression is an important structure of a text, and it serves as an important means to maintain cohesion and coherence and to control information flow in the text. Every text can be regarded as a sequence of themes, presented in the form of mutual connections and gradual progression of themes, and "with the progression of themes in the clauses, the text unfolds itself gradually till it forms a whole one capable of expressing some complete textual meaning." (Zhu et al. 2001:102-103)

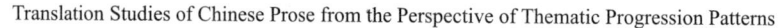

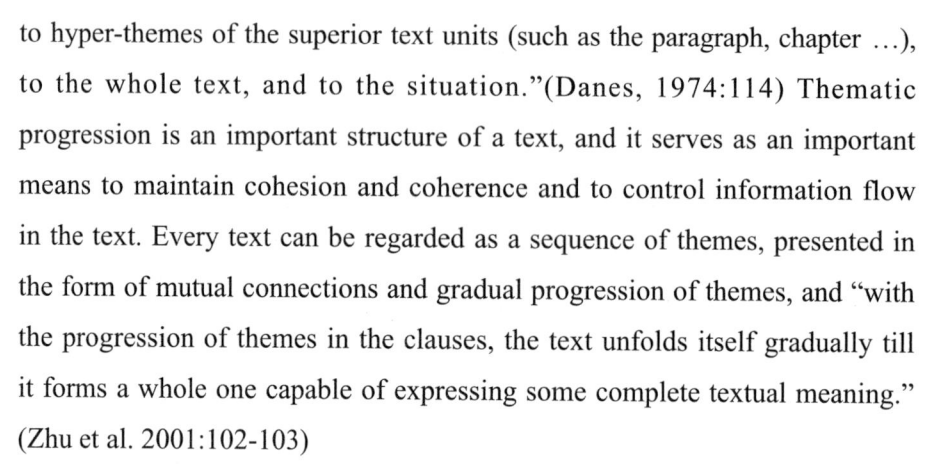

As far as functions of TP in textual translation are concerned, Hatim (2001:80-85) points out that "the notion of Thematic Progression is a potentially useful analytic tool for unlocking texts and revealing their texture", and he also combines TP patterns with text type for analysis. Papegaaij & Schubert (1988) hold that proper thematic progression contributes to constructing a coherent translated text. Wang (2000:35-37) is the first researcher at home to discuss translation issues from the perspective of thematic progression. He discovers the constructing function of thematic progression in translating from Chinese to English and its deconstructing function in translating from English to Chinese. Zhao et al. (2003:76-80) focus on how to strengthen the cohesion and coherence of a text at both the structural level and the grammatical and lexical level in Chinese-English textual translation and maintain that patterns of TP help to construct the structural framework of the target text and cohesive devices contribute to achieving semantic connections and coherence of the text, so they should be combined in Chinese-English translation.

Translation refers to the transference between two languages on the basis of semantic meanings. The thematic progression formed by the interaction of themes and rhemes can realize the surface connections of the text, while the deep connections of the text should be reflected in its semantic coherence. Therefore, approaching textual translation from the perspective of thematic progression should combine the formal connections achieved through thematic progression with implicit semantic coherence of the text.

2.2.4 Researches on Transference of TP Patterns in Textual Translation

Although there are various types and genres of texts, and the connections between themes and rhemes vary from text to text, TP in a text still has certain patterns to follow. Many scholars at home and abroad have summarized their respective kinds of TP patterns on the basis of their investigations on textual structure in English as well as other languages. Danes (1974:118-119) firstly put forward five common kinds of TP patterns, and from then up to the present, the frequently-mentioned classifications of TP patterns proposed in succession by researchers are as follows: four types put forward by Xu (1982:3-4); seven types by Huang (1985:34-35); six types by Huang (1988:81-85); three types by Hu (1994:144-145); and four types by Zhu (1995:7). In generally, the connections between themes and rhemes of clauses in a piece of text move forward in line with one of the above-mentioned patterns or some mixed patterns.

TP patterns are the forms of arranging the linguistic materials in a text, and they are the important means in fulfilling the textual functions, for they are of help not only to writers in producing their texts but also to translators in interpreting the texts. TP patterns display the framework and overall orientation of a text and reflect the author's methods and rhetorical intentions of creating the text, so they serve as an important reference for translators in understanding the source text as well as reproducing the target text, hence an important factor worthy of notice in textual translation.

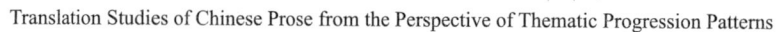

Studies have shown that, in general, translators have maintained the TP patterns of the source text in the target text, because the translators tend to copy the TP patterns of the original text, consciously or unconsciously, in translation practice. The translation should be as consistent as possible with the original text in terms of TP patterns. Of course, this does not mean that the translators should imitate the TP patterns of the source text at the expense of the semantic coherence of the target text. The preservation of TP patterns should be based on the premise of not disrupting the target text. Because English and Chinese belong to different language families, both of them have their own special characteristics in syntactic structure and expression, which will affect the preservation of the TP patterns of the original text in translation to a certain extent. In view of the differences between English and Chinese, in the cases where the TP patterns of the original text cannot be preserved in translation, the TP patterns of the target text should be properly adjusted or reconstructed on the premise of conforming to the target language norms.

Since TP patterns serve as an important textual resource for a translator, how to transfer them properly in textual translation has attracted much attention from researchers. Ventola (1995:85-104) explores the transference of TP patterns in the translation of technical texts between English and German. Hatim & Mason (2001:217-222) argue that "the patterns (of TP) are always employed in the service of an overriding rhetorical purpose. This is an aspect of texture which is of crucial importance to the translator." They also combine TP patterns with text genre, arguing that "there is a preference for a given pattern in a given text plan" and the translator should be aware of this in translation practice. Zhang (2006:22-26) claims that in translating fictions, keeping the TP patterns of the original text means more than achieving cohesion and coherence of the translated text, because the peculiarity of literary texts often enables their TP patterns to embody the author's poetic intentions and aesthetic inclinations. Therefore, in translating novels, preserving the TP patterns of the original text is not only conducive to constructing a coherent text and creating artistic effects which are similar to the source text, but also helps to convey the author's poetic intentions in the target text. Liu (2006:309-312) holds that TP patterns of clauses in a text generally embody its textual purpose and textual effect, so in textual translation, TP patterns of the source text should be reproduced or restructured in the target text so as to achieve the same textual purpose and at least the similar overall textual effect. However, Liu(2006:310) admits that "in a strict sense, the possibility of keeping the TP patterns of English texts in their Chinese renderings is slim." In the cases where the TP patterns of the source text cannot be retained, the translator should conform to the thematic progression norms of the target language in order to construct a properly cohesive and semantically coherent target text and reproduce the communicative effects of the source text.

From the current results of relevant research, we can summarize three types of transference of TP patterns in terms of English-Chinese translation, that is, preserving, adjusting and reconstructing the patterns of thematic progression in the target text. It should be noted that the application of TP patterns to text-based translation studies up to the present mostly focuses on theoretical speculations supported by some illustrative examples. However, this kind of research is inadequate and unfavorable for us to observe accurately and describe effectively the phenomena of transference of TP patterns actually occurring in the translation process.

Although fruits of research have been reaped in applying theme-based theories to text-oriented translation studies, which has deepened our understanding of the translating process in this regard, it should be pointed out that empirical study in this field remains relatively unexplored, which is disadvantageous for researchers to observe and discover laws of transference in textual translation based on large-scale data. Therefore, further research in this respect needs to be conducted and it is necessary to shift our research approach from a prescriptive one to a descriptive one and to conduct a careful and detailed description of the transference of thematic structure and TP patterns in textual translation under the framework of Descriptive Translation Studies. We should first select language materials properly, the amount of which should be large enough to ensure an adequate observation; and then conduct statistical analyses and systematic classifications of all the transference, regular and irregular, appearing in the translated texts to guarantee an adequate description; and finally explain both regular and irregular transference on the basis of the above-mentioned two steps, observe the laws of transference, and reveal various underlying constraints to ensure an adequate interpretation. Based on the adequate observation, description and explanation, we can deepen our understanding of the laws of the transference in textual translation and verify these laws in the translation practice. By doing so, we can definitely promote the development of studies in this field.

Chapter 3

Thematic Progression and Literary Text Analysis

An excellent literary work is attractive not only because of its plot and content carefully woven by the author, but also because of the beautiful and exquisite language in the work. Finding an appropriate form of linguistic expression for the content of their literary works is what many writers long for, which calls for their meditation. Therefore, the analysis of literary works can be done not just from the perspective of its content but also from its form. In terms of a literary work, the content is embodied by the form, by means of which its content can be realized. Apart from that, the form itself often implies the literary meaning and reflects the literariness of the work. Patterns of thematic progression serve as an important means of text generation, for they embody the textual meanings of a text and reflect the way conceptual and interpersonal meanings of the text are organized from one aspect. As a result, patterns of thematic progression are widely used in textual analysis, and many scholars conduct their researches on them from the viewpoint of specific types of text, such as discussions on the application of TP patterns in analyzing scientific and technical texts, advertisement texts, journalistic texts, medical texts, etc. However, studies on the application of TP patterns in analyzing literary texts are still rarely seen. Up till now, there exists only a few relevant research papers in this regard. Li Guoqing (2003:53-56) explores the relationship between patterns of thematic progression and text genres through a case study of the novel entitled "*The Old Man and the Sea*", and Zhang Man (2005:1-3) discusses the variation and coherence of TP patterns in stream-of-consciousness novels. In view of this situation, we intend to probe into the application of thematic progression patterns in literary text analysis here.

3.1 Common Patterns of Thematic Progression

According to actual division of the sentence proposed by V. Mathesius, the founder of Prague School, every sentence can be divided from the viewpoint of its communicative functions into two semantic components: Theme and Rheme. The idea was later accepted and developed by M. A. K. Halliday, the master of Systemic Functional Linguistics. Halliday (2000:37) and Thompson (2000:119) both hold that "as a message structure, a clause consists of a Theme accompanied by a Rheme". "The Theme is the element which serves as the point of departure of the message; it is that with which the clause is concerned." (Halliday, 2000:37) That is to say, the theme of a clause is simply the first constituent of the clause, and all the rest of the clause is simply called the rheme, the part in which the theme is developed. Theme is an important concept in describing clause structure under the background of text. Theme always lies at the beginning of a clause, starting from the beginning of the clause and ending with the topic theme. The component of a clause serving as the theme should be a component of the transitivity system of the clause, such as participant, process, or environmental element.

When a series of meaningful clauses develop into a piece of coherent text, the themes and rhemes of these clauses will inter-connect with each other and contribute to the flow of information in the text. The inter-connections between these themes and rhemes are termed as Thematic Progression (TP). The concept of "thematic progression" is initially put forward by Czech linguist F. Danes (1974:114). TP is an important structure of a text, and it serves as an important means to maintain cohesion and coherence and to control information flow in the text. Every text can be regarded as a sequence of themes, presented in the form of mutual connections and gradual progression of themes, and "with the progression of themes in the clauses, the text unfolds itself gradually till it forms a whole one capable of expressing some complete meaning." (Zhu et al. 2001:102-103)

Although there are various types and genres of texts, and the connections between themes and rhemes vary from text to text, TP in a text still has certain patterns to follow. Scholars at home and abroad have summarized their respective kinds of TP patterns on the basis of their investigations on textual structure in English as well as other languages. Danes (1974:118-119) firstly put forward five common kinds of TP patterns, and from then up to the present, the frequently-mentioned classifications of TP patterns proposed in succession by researchers are as follows: four types put forward by Xu (1982:3-4); seven types by Huang (1985:34-35); six types by Huang (1988:81-85); three types by Hu (1994:144-145); and four types by Zhu (1995:7). We adopt the notion of "thematic progression" defined by Danes and find out the following kinds of TP patterns based on our initial observations of textual structures in some literary texts, with the previous classifications of TP patterns proposed by various scholars as the frame of reference. (Note: T and R stand for Theme and Rheme respectively in all the examples listed in this book.)

1. TP with a constant theme, which means a series of clauses have the same theme but different rhemes, and these rhemes develop around the same theme from different angles. For example,

(1) Revolution (T_1) is bloody and hostile (R_1). Revolution (T_2) knows no compromise (R_2). Revolution (T_3) overturns and destroys everything that gets

in its way (R_3).

2. TP with derived themes, which means the themes of other clauses are derived from the theme of the first clause in a set of clauses. For example,

(2) Three children (T_1) are playing in the courtyard (R_1). The girl in red (T_2) is chasing a butterfly (R_2). The younger girl (T_3) is patting a ball (R_3), and the boy (T_4) is riding a bike (R_4).

3. TP with a continuous rheme, which means a series of clauses have the same rheme but different themes, and these themes are all concentrated on the same rheme. For example,

(3) Father (T_1) gave him a present (R_1). Mother (T_2) gave him a present (R_2). Uncle Jim (T_3) gave him a present (R_3). We (T_4) all gave him presents (R_4) for his birthday.

4. TP with a split rheme, which means the rheme of the first clause splits into several semantic elements to serve as themes of the subsequent clauses in a set of clauses. For example,

(4) Studies (T_1) serve for delight, for ornament, and for ability (R_1). Their chief use for delight (T_2), is in privateness and retiring (R_2); for ornament (T_3), is in discourse (R_3); and for ability (T_4), is in the judgement and disposition of business (R_4).

5. Linear TP, which means the rheme of the preceding clause becomes the theme of the following clause, and this theme introduces a new rheme in a series of clauses. For example,

(5) Outside my window (T_1) is a big lawn (R_1). In the middle of the lawn (T_2) is a flower bed (R_2). This bed (T_3) is full of daffodils (R_3).

6. Crisscrossed TP, which means the theme of the preceding clause grows into the rheme of the following clause in a series of clauses. For example,

(6) The play (T_1) was interesting (R_1), but I (T_2) didn't enjoy it (R_2). A

young man and a young woman (T$_3$) troubled me (R$_3$). I (T$_4$) turned around and looked at them (R$_4$), but they (T$_5$) didn't pay any attention to me (R$_5$).

7. TP with two alternate themes, which means two different themes appear alternately, and their respective rhemes make corresponding changes in a set of clauses. For example,

(7) Americans (T$_1$) eat with knives and forks (R$_1$); Japanese (T$_2$) eat with chopsticks (R$_2$). Americans (T$_3$) say "Hi" (R$_3$) when they meet; Japanese (T$_4$) bow (R$_4$). Many American men (T$_5$) open doors for women (R$_5$); Japanese men (T$_6$) do not (R$_6$).

Generally speaking, the connections between themes and rhemes of clauses in a piece of text move forward in line with one of the above-mentioned patterns or some mixed patterns. Three points have to be made clear here. Firstly, when a clause employs the theme or rheme of the preceding clause, it does not necessarily copy them word for word, but it usually resorts to part of their semantic substance, or it may develop or change their original semantic contents to some extent. Secondly, these afore-mentioned patterns are merely the basic TP patterns to describe the development of a text. In the practical language use, it happens frequently that several patterns tend to work together in a text in order to express a complicated idea or event. The overall TP patterns in a text are the organic combination of these basic patterns, each pattern playing a certain role in the overall framework of the text. Thirdly, The above-mentioned seven patterns are the most basic ones of thematic progression in texts. In some other literary texts, variations of TP patterns may also occur. For example, there are intermittent TP, TP with inserted elements and TP with no regular pattern in stream-of-consciousness novels (Zhang, 2005:1-3), which reflect the special writing techniques of this kind of novels. Thematic Progression is invented to study how Theme in a text is developed from clause to clause or larger stretches of text. TP plays an important role in maintaining coherence in text and it is closely related to the method of development in text. TP patterns are the forms of arranging the linguistic materials in a text, and they are the important means in fulfilling the textual functions, for they are of help not only to writers in producing their texts but also to readers in understanding the literary texts. TP patterns display the framework and overall orientation of a text and reflect the author's methods and rhetorical intentions of creating the text, so they serve as an important tool in textual analysis.

3.2 Application of TP Patterns in Literary Text Analysis

Different patterns of thematic progression reflect different development methods of textual information. Any text will show a certain pattern of thematic progression, and literary text is no exception. The patterns of thematic progression in literary texts serve as one of the important means to realize the literariness of the literary works. Hidden behind them are often the author's poetic intentions and the special aesthetic effects of the literary works. Understanding and analyzing the patterns of thematic progression is helpful for readers to analyze the semantic structure of literary texts, so as to get an accurate understanding of the content of the text. It is also helpful for us to grasp the framework of literary texts, the development modes and direction of textual information flow, as well as the author's intentions, so as to interpret the text more quickly and accurately. As far as a specific literary text is concerned, we can firstly divide each of the sentences in the text, one by one, into the theme and the rheme, and then discover the patterns of thematic progression adopted by the text. By doing so, we can figure out the author's thoughts according to the textual framework embodied in the patterns of thematic progression, and thus to understand the author's writing intentions as well as the semantic contents of the text. In the following part, we will explore the application of TP patterns in literary text analysis with specific examples.

(8) A good book (T_1) may be among the best of friends (R_1). It (T_2) is the same today that it always was (R_2), and it (T_3) will never change (R_3). It (T_4) is the most patient and cheerful of companions (R_4). It (T_5) does not turn its back upon us in time of adversity or distress (R_5). It (T_6) always receives us with the same kindness, amusing and instructing us in youth, and comforting and consoling us age (R_6). ("*Companionship of Books*" by Samuel Smiles, Gao, 2001:316)

The pattern of thematic progression employed in Example(8) is a typical TP with a constant theme. All the six clauses are unfolded around the same theme (a good book) with different rhemes. By analyzing the patterns of thematic progression in the text, we can better grasp the author's textual intention, that is, expounding the view that "A good book may be among the best of friends" from different perspectives.

(9) Nothing (T_1) can be more imposing than the magnificence of English park scenery (R_1). Vast lawns (T_2) that extend like sheets of vivid green, with here and there clumps of gigantic trees heaping up rich piles of foliage (R_2); the solemn pomp of groves and woodland glades (T_3) with the deer trooping in silent herds across them, the hare bounding away to the covert, or the pheasant suddenly bursting upon the wing (R_3); the brook (T_4), taught to wind in natural meanderings or expand into a glassy lake (R_4); the sequestered pool (T_5), reflecting the quivering trees, with the yellow leaf sleeping on its bosom, and the trout roaming fearlessly about its limpid waters (R_5); while some rustic

temple or sylvan statue (T_6), grown green and dank with age, gives an air of classic sanctity to the seclusion (R_6). ("*Rural Life in England*" by Washington Irving, Gao, 2001:238)

The pattern of thematic progression used in Example(9) is a typical TP with a split rheme. The rheme(English park scenery)of the first clause which appears at a higher level subdivides and becomes the themes of the following five clauses. The author first points out that the magnificence of English park scenery is unparalleled in the world, and then shows readers an imposing English park scenery through detailed descriptions (vast lawns, groves and woodland glades, the brook, the sequestered pool, some rustic temple or sylvan statue).

(10) The style of Dryden (T_1) is capricious and varied (R_1), that of Pope (T_2) is cautious and uniform (R_2); Dryden (T_3) obeys the motions of his own mind (R_3), Pope (T_4) constrains his mind to his own rules of composition (R_4). Dryden (T_5) is sometimes vehement and rapid (R_5); Pope (T_6) is always smooth, uniform and gentile (R_6). Dryden's page (T_7) is a natural field, rising into inequalities, and diversified by the varied exuberance of abundant vegetation (R_7); Pope's (T_8) is a velvet lawn, shaven by the scythe, and leveled by the roller (R_8). ("*The Lives of the English Poets: Pope*" by Samuel Johnson, Gao, 2001:142)

In Example(10), the author successfully constructs the text by resorting to TP with two alternate themes. Through the alternation of two different themes (Dryden and Pope), the author makes a comprehensive comparison of the prose styles of Pope and Dryden from various aspects, which refer to the rhemes that change correspondingly with the themes of these clauses. TP with two alternate themes is often used to compare and analyze the differences between two things.

In all the above-mentioned three examples, only one pattern of thematic progression is employed to organize textual information for each text. Generally speaking, a literary text does not simply follow a certain pattern of thematic progression from the beginning to the end. Because the complexity of human thinking cannot be clearly expressed by one pattern of thematic progression in most cases, most texts are the result of an integration of multiple TP patterns, among which one pattern is often more prominent than others.

(11) The family of Dashwood (T_1) had been long settled in Sussex (R_1). Their estate (T_2) was large (R_2), and their residence (T_3) was at Norland Park, in the centre of their property, where, for many generations, they had lived in so respectable a manner as to engage the general good opinion of their surrounding acquaintance (R_3). The late owner of this estate (T_4) was a single man who lived to a very advanced age, and who for many years of his life had a constant companion and housekeeper in his sister (R_4). But her death, which happened ten years before his own (T_5), produced a great alteration in his home (R_5); for to supply her loss (T_6), he invited and received into his house the family of his nephew Mr. Henry Dashwood, the legal inheritor of the Norland estate, and the person to whom he intended to bequeath it (R_6). In the society of his nephew and niece, and their children (T_7), the old gentleman's days were comfortably spent (R_7). His attachment to them all (T_8) increased (R_8). The constant attention of Mr. and Mrs. Henry Dashwood to his wishes, which proceeded not merely from interest, but from goodness of heart (T_9), gave him every degree of solid comfort which his age could receive (R_9); and the cheerfulness of the children (T_{10}) added a relish to his existence (R_{10}). ("*Sense and Sensitivity*" by Jane Austen, 2007:3)

Example(11) is the opening part of the well-known novel entitled *Sense and Sensitivity* by Jane Austen, a famous British writer. Here the author makes an integrated use of several patterns such as TP with derived themes (between T_1 and T_2, T_3, between T_7 and T_9, T_{10}), TP with a constant theme (between T_2 and T_4, between T_5 and T_6) and simple linear TP (between R_4 and T_5, between R_6 and T_7, and between R_7 and T_8). As the beginning part of a novel, the author generally needs to introduce some characters and briefly describe some background information of the story, so as to pave the way for the development of the novel in the following chapters. In order to clearly express the complex relationship between these characters and events, the author employs more than one pattern of thematic progression in this text. The use of TP with a constant theme and TP with derived themes enables the author to give a complete account of the characters and background involved, while the use of simple linear TP ensures the smoothness of the narrative, jointly making this text a part of the literary masterpiece. By analyzing the patterns of thematic progression in this text, we can grasp the content and structure of the text quickly and accurately, get an initial understanding of the characters and background of the novel, and appreciate the author's method of organizing the text information.

Since the analysis of TP patterns in the text is based on the segmentation of a clause into theme and rheme, there will inevitably be some limitations. In order to describe and analyze patterns of thematic progression in a text from a higher level, the Systemic Functional linguist Martin (1992:437) proposed another two concepts for the first time, namely, paragraph-based hyper-theme and text-based macro-theme, in addition to the concept of theme, which is defined on the basis of clause. These two concepts are respectively equivalent to topic sentence and introductory paragraph in rhetoric. Macro-theme heralds the emergence of hyper-theme. Accordingly, hyper-theme heralds the emergence of a series of themes of the clauses. Given that sometimes a paragraph is composed of more than one sentence group, and the semantic contents expressed by this paragraph cannot be wholly covered by a hyper-theme, it seems necessary to introduce a new concept of super-theme, which is based on a sentence group. Super-theme refers to the syntactic components that can command, from the semantic point of view, a series of themes or both themes and rhemes of a group of clauses. It is actually the theme of a sentence group, which can appear at the beginning or the end of a series of clauses. In short, the progression of a series of clause-based themes results in a super-theme, the progression of some sentence-group-based super-themes constitutes the hyper-theme, and the progression of a few paragraph-based hyper-themes finally reflects the macro-theme of a text. The following paragraph is provided here to exemplify the role of super-theme in literary text analysis.

(12) Five score years ago (T_1), a great American, in whose symbolic shadow we stand today, signed the *Emancipation Proclamation* (R_1). This momentous decree (T_2) came as a great beacon light of hope to millions of Negro slaves who had been seared in the flames of withering injustice (R_2). It (T_3) came as a joyous daybreak to end the long night of their captivity (R_3). But one hundred years later (T_4), the Negro still is not free (R_4). One hundred years later (T_5), the life of the Negro is still sadly crippled by the manacles of segregation and the chains of discrimination (R_5). One hundred years later (T_6), the Negro lives on a lonely island of poverty in the midst of a vast ocean of material prosperity (R_6). One hundred years later (T_7), the Negro is still anguished in the corners of American society and finds himself in exile in his shameful condition (R_7). ("*I Have a Dream*" by Martin Luther King Jr.)

Example(12) is a part of a wonderful speech, in which the author mainly makes use of simple linear TP (between R_1 and T_2) and TP with a constant theme (between T_2 and T_3, between T_4 and T_5, T_6 and T_7). Here, the repeated use of TP with a constant theme effectively enhances the textual effect. By means of this formal device, the author successfully achieves the purpose of this text, that is, denouncing the evil of racism in the United States and expressing his yearning for a truly free and equal society. Through the analysis of the clause-based segmentation of theme and rheme as well as the patterns of thematic progression, and then to understand the content of the text, we can find that the text is composed of two sentence groups, and their super-themes are respectively five score years ago (T_1) and one hundred years later (T_4). These two super-themes semantically dominate the content of the subsequent series of clauses and constitute the structural framework of this paragraph. The author here uses the textual information organized by two super-themes of the two sentence groups to compare the hopes and visions of Black Americans a hundred years ago and the tragic situation of them in American society a hundred years later. By identifying and analyzing the super-themes of sentence groups in this paragraph, we can grasp the semantic structure and contents of the text from a higher level. In doing text analysis, combining the analysis of TP patterns based on clauses with the analysis of sentence-group-based super-themes at a higher level can help us better understand and analyze the text.

Due to space limitations, no more examples will be provided here. According to our observation of the literary texts, some conclusions can be arrived at. Firstly, in general, patterns of TP are more complicated in literary texts than in other types of texts, and in most cases several patterns of TP are combined to produce a literary text, while the use of a single TP pattern is rarely seen. The reason for this phenomenon is that literary texts usually express more intricate thoughts and relationships, and as far as literary texts are concerned, the form itself is particularly important, for it carries both the content and meanings of the text and poetic intentions of the author. The patterns of thematic progression, often used as an important formal means of literary text generation, are bound to be flexible so as to effectively express complex ideas. Secondly, TP with a constant theme, TP with derived themes, TP with a split rheme and simple linear TP are the most frequently employed ones in literary texts. That is because the author will inevitably elaborate and explain a certain thing from different angles in order to emphasize a certain point of view or describe something in a detailed manner, thus using frequently TP with a constant theme. Sometimes, in order to make the point of view prominent and the arrangement of ideas clear, the author will firstly put forward a general viewpoint or outline the characters and events, and then demonstrate and describe them through a large number of details, as is often the case when describing the characters in the novel. By doing so, the author will usually use TP with derived themes and TP with a split rheme more often than other patterns of TP. In order to make the text information flow smoothly and fluently in narration, the author often starts from the given information in the previous sentence and brings out new information. This method of writing will enable the author to achieve an orderly development of text information and a desirable arrangement of ideas, hence he is inclined to use simple linear TP more frequently to organize the text. Thirdly, due to the various styles of literary works of different authors and their respective preferences for the choice of words and organizations in expressing ideas, the author's choice of TP patterns in producing literary texts will also be affected.

Information of a text is gradually unfolded through various patterns of thematic progression. The particularity of literary texts often enables the patterns of thematic progression to carry the poetic intention and aesthetic tendency of the author. From the above-mentioned analysis, it can be seen that patterns of thematic progression play an important role both in writers' construction of and in readers' analysis of literary texts. Appropriate patterns of thematic progression can help authors achieve their textual purpose and poetic intentions. The use of TP patterns to analyze literary texts can help readers to achieve a better understanding of the content of the texts as well as the author's methods of organizing textual information, and it is also helpful for us to appreciate the charm of excellent literary works. There is no denying that patterns of thematic progression are only one of the different ways in literary text analysis. The analysis of literary texts can be carried out from a variety of angles to make up for the shortcomings of this formal analysis method.

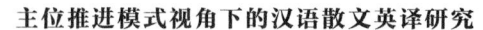

Chapter 4

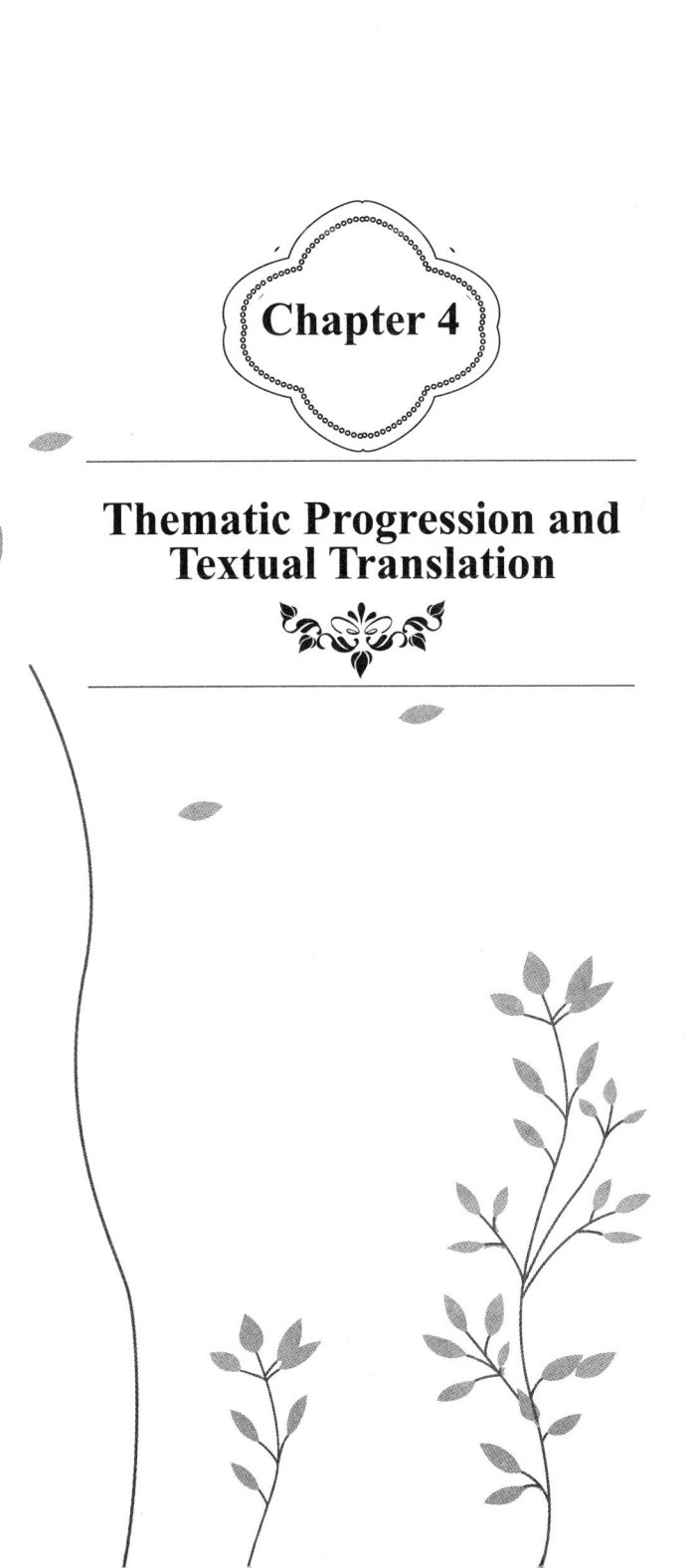

Thematic Progression and Textual Translation

4.1 Descriptive Approach to Translation Studies

Toury (2001:1) points out clearly that "it (translation studies) is therefore empirical by its very nature and should be worked out accordingly." By "empirical science or discipline" we mean conducting research on the basis of observation, scientific experiment or practical experience of phenomena in the real world rather than theory or pure logic. Therefore, in the first place, "what constitutes the subject matter of a proper discipline of Translation Studies is (observable or reconstructable) facts of real life rather than merely speculative entities resulting from preconceived hypotheses and theoretical models." (Toury, 2001:1) and in the second place, "describing, explaining and predicting phenomena pertaining to its object level is thus the main goal of such a discipline." (ibid:1)

As an empirical discipline, translation studies has two main objectives: "1) to describe the phenomena of translating and translation(s) as they manifest themselves in the world of our experience, and 2) to establish general principles by means of which these phenomena can be explained and predicted." (Holmes, 1988:71) Observations and descriptions of phenomena in the existing translated texts provide the necessary data and form the basis on which the theory of translation can be formulated, because "the cumulative findings of descriptive studies should make it possible to formulate a series of coherent *laws* which would state the inherent relations between all the variables found to be relevant to translation." (Toury, 2001:16, emphasis original)

Toury attaches great importance to the roles of descriptive studies with regard to an empirical discipline, claiming that "no empirical science can make a claim for completeness and (relative) autonomy unless it has a proper *descriptive branch*." (Toury, 2001:1, emphasis original) He lays emphasis on the "pivotal" position of the branch of Descriptive Translation Studies (DTS) in the whole framework of Translation Studies (TS) because DTS, based on the translational phenomena in the objective world, can not only offer materials and evidence in the formulation of laws in the branch of Theoretical Translation Studies (TTS), but also bridge the gap between Translation Theory (TT) and the applied extensions of Translation Studies. The key point of Descriptive Translation Studies is describing the existing phenomena of translation in an objective and all-round way, analyzing various conditioning factors behind these phenomena, and drawing conclusions of universal significance with the hope of predicting translational phenomena in the future.

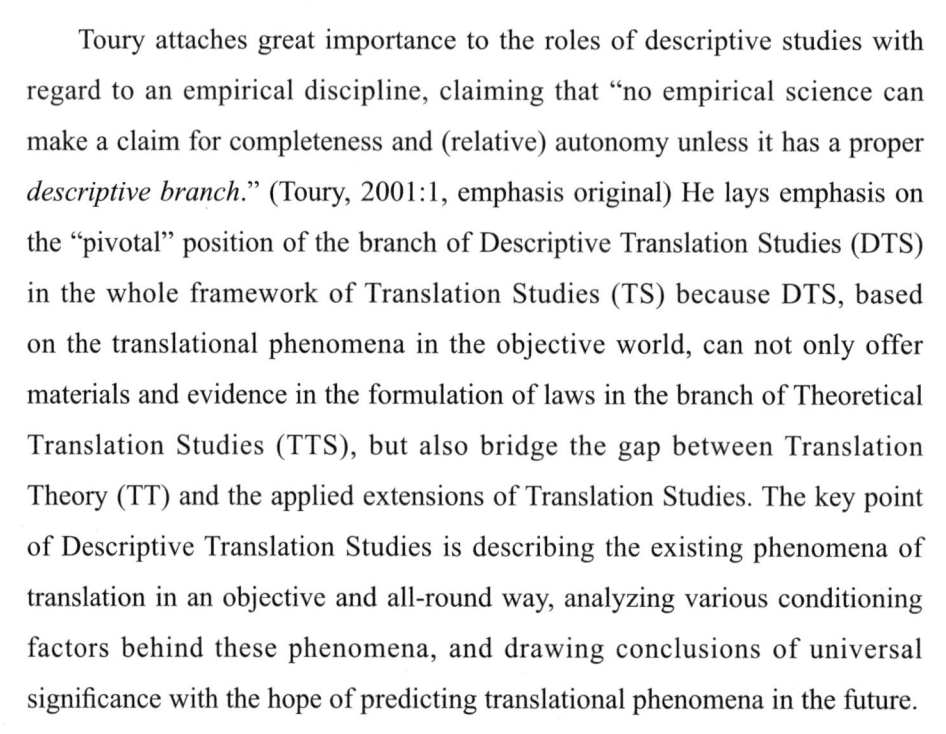

It is the essential requirement of Descriptive Translation Studies to approach translation issues from the existing translational phenomena and to test the current theoretical models and hypotheses with the conclusions acquired from systematic descriptions and explanations of these phenomena. For this reason, textual translation studies from the descriptive approach should first of all give a detailed description of large numbers of existing translated texts, because "only on the basis of translated texts can we explore laws of translation and expound the translated texts in a systematic way, can we revise and improve translation theories and make translation studies more normalized and scientific." (Fang, 2001:23) and then probe into the laws or universals of translation inherent in the translated texts on the basis of linguistic and textual features exhibited in them. To put it specifically, this approach involves putting forward research questions and hypotheses, collecting and classifying relevant data, conducting descriptions and statistical analyses, explaining the results of data processing from the theoretical perspective, testing and revising hypotheses, and finally summarizing laws.

To conduct a careful and meaningful description of the transference of TP patterns in textual translation under the framework of Descriptive Translation Studies, we should 1) select language materials properly, the amount of which should be large enough to ensure an adequate observation; and 2) conduct statistical analyses and systematic classifications of all the transference, regular and irregular, appearing in the translated texts to guarantee an adequate description; and 3) explain both regular and irregular transference on the basis of the above two steps, observe the laws of transference, and reveal various underlying constraints to ensure an adequate interpretation. Based on the adequate observation, description and explanation, we can deepen our understanding of the laws of the transference in textual translation and verify these laws in our translation practice.

4.2 Patterns of Thematic Progression in Texts

4.2.1 Definition of Theme

Theme is an important concept in Systemic Functional Grammar. "Theme is the starting-point for the message; it is the ground from which the clause is taking off." (Halliday, 2000:38) Once the Theme is identified, all the rest of the clause is simply labeled the Rheme. Halliday (2000:38) holds that "as a general guide, the Theme can be identified as that element which comes in first position in the clause. ... this is not how the category of Theme is defined. The definition is functional, ..." (emphasis original) At the same time, Halliday (2000:38) points out that "first position in the clause is not what defines the Theme; it is the means whereby the function of Theme is realized, in the grammar of English." (emphasis original) Jiang (2008:137-146) reviews the evolution of the notion of theme in Systemic Functional Grammar through detailed examination of the definitions given by Halliday in the past decades or so, and argues that 1) theme and given information are two different notions, although they are often realized by the same element in unmarked situations; 2) theme has been kept apart from what the message is about, i.e. the notion of aboutness; and 3) it's not appropriate to simply equate theme with the initial position of a clause.

In our opinion, it is more defendable to keep to the functional notion of theme, that is, to define theme as "the starting-point for the message" in a clause, and to make a clear distinction between the functional notion of theme and the formal notion of theme as "the initial element of a clause". The element which is put at the initial position of a clause is not necessarily the theme, so we should "distinguish between elements which always come initially in a clause and those placed there as a thematic choice." (Jiang, 2008:144) Adhering to this principle shows much significance in guiding our identification of themes of clauses in the data.

The theme together with the rheme composes the thematic structure, which is based on the unit of a clause. Themes generally fall into three types: simple themes, multiple themes, and clausal themes. The theme always lies in the beginning of a clause and extends from here up to the element called the topical theme. The theme always contains one, and only one, experiential element, which can be either participant, process, or circumstance in the system of transitivity.

The significance of research on theme and thematic structure lies in the fact that they can help us understand the distribution of information and its communicative functions in utterances as well as the internal structure of a clause. Actually, every text can be treated as a succession of themes, presented in the form of mutual connections and gradual progression of themes. The choice of themes determines the starting point of information in a text and the orientation of it. The interactions of themes and rhemes in a text form appropriate TP patterns, which display the structural framework of the text and effectively convey the information in the text. Theme also plays a constructive role in connecting the sentences around the clause in which it appears, so an author can often guide the readers in their interpretation of the text through his deliberate choice of those elements serving as themes in the text.

4.2.2 Definition of Thematic Progression

When a series of meaningful clauses develop into a piece of coherent text, the themes and rhemes of these clauses will inter-connect with each other and contribute to the flow of information in the text. The inter-connections between these themes and rhemes are termed as Thematic Progression. It is firstly proposed by linguist Danes, which he defines as "the choice and ordering of utterance themes, their mutual concatenation and hierarchy, as well as their relationship to hyper-themes of the superior text units (such as the paragraph, chapter ...), to the whole text, and to the situation."(Danes, 1974:114) Moreover, "thematic progression exhibits the frame of textual structure." (Huang, 1988:80)

TP is an important structure of a text, and it serves as an important means to maintain cohesion and coherence and to control information flow in the text because "it links up information in the text in a good order and leads to smooth transition from a clause to the next one." (Wang, 2000:35) Every text can be regarded as a sequence of themes, presented in the form of mutual connections and gradual progression of themes, and "with the progression of themes in the clauses, the text unfolds itself gradually till it forms a whole one capable of expressing some complete meaning." (Zhu et al., 2001:102-103)

4.2.3 Classification of TP Patterns

Although there are various types and genres of texts, and the connections between themes and rhemes vary from text to text, TP in a text still has certain patterns to follow. Scholars at home and abroad have summarized different kinds of TP patterns on the basis of their investigations on textual structure in English as well as other languages. We adopt the notion of "thematic progression" defined by Danes and find out the following 14 kinds of TP patterns based on our observations of textual structures in all the selected Chinese and English texts, with the previous classifications of TP patterns proposed by various scholars as the frame of reference.

Generally speaking, the connections between themes and rhemes of clauses in a piece of text move forward in line with one of the above-mentioned patterns or some mixed patterns. Two points have to be made clear here. Firstly, when a clause employs the theme or rheme of the preceding clause, it does not necessarily copy them word for word, but it usually resorts to part of their semantic substance, or it may develop or change their original semantic contents to some extent. Secondly, these afore-mentioned patterns are merely the basic TP patterns to describe the development of a text. In the practical language use, it happens frequently that several patterns tend to work together in a text in order to express a complicated idea or event. The overall TP patterns in a text are the organic combination of these basic patterns, each pattern playing a certain role in the overall framework of the text.

4.2.4 Differences of Thematic Structure Between Chinese and English

According to the new linguistic typology advanced by American linguists Charles Li and Sandra Thompson (Li, 1976; Li & Thompson, 1981), English is a subject-prominent language whereas Chinese is a topic-prominent language. The themes of clauses in English are mostly overlapped with the subjects of the clauses. In English, "there tends to be a very high correlation between theme / rheme and subject / predicate in the Halliday an model. The correlation does not hold in the case of marked themes, but, generally speaking, the distinction between theme and rheme is more or less identical to the traditional grammatical distinction between subject and predicate." (Baker, 2000:123)

However, the clauses in Chinese are generally lacking such explicit formal features as displayed clearly in English clauses, and they are often organized into a text on the basis of their inner meanings. Those clauses with comments centering around a topic abound in Chinese. "A clause in Chinese is essentially a semantic structure typical of 'topic + comment', and the theme in a clause is virtually the topic of it." (Li, 2001:200) Moreover, one feature of topic in the Chinese language is that "once an element is announced as topic, this element may be omitted altogether in subsequent clauses, hence the proliferation of subjectless clauses …" (Baker, 2000:142) Moreover, the theme in the Chinese language is not confined to the clause, sometimes there appears both theme at the clause level and topic at the sentence level. The differences in thematic structure between English and Chinese pose delicate problems for a translator and call for his discretion in the process of textual translation between the two languages.

4.3 Thematic Progression in Textual Translation

4.3.1 Theme and Textual Translation

Transference between two languages in the process of translating is generally conducted at the clause level, so the theory of theme, which is clause-based, is of great significance to a translator in analyzing, transferring and constructing clauses as well as ensuring cohesion and coherence of text in textual translation. Therefore, it is easy to handle for a translator to take theme as the unit of textual translation in his translating action. A translator can understand the distribution of information in the clauses through analysis of their themes and rhemes and their functions in the text, on the basis of which he can conduct transference between two languages. Furthermore, the choice of elements serving as themes will have some effect on the structure of clauses and consequently on the cohesion and coherence of the translated text.

Since theme and thematic structure are of much use in decoding the source text and encoding the target text, it is ideal in English-Chinese translation for a translator to be able to keep the thematic structure of the source text. However, we cannot always manage to do that in the actual situation as we have expected because the two languages have its distinctive ways of expression and different clause structures, so a translator should conform to the norms and habits of linguistic expression in different languages and conduct proper transference of thematic structure.

4.3.2 Thematic Progression and Textual Translation

With the rise of text linguistics and its application to translation studies, text is gradually becoming the focus in the theory and practice of translation both at home and abroad. Among the several textual features mentioned by Halliday (2000:334), structural textual features (i.e. thematic structure and information structure) are particularly important for the effective transmission of information. Many scholars such as Liu et al. (2000:61-66) and Li (2002:19-22) have discussed the application of the concept of theme in translation studies. Theme is put forward, under the background of text analysis, as an important concept for describing the structure of a clause, and it is based on clause. However, it is the text, not just one single clause after another, that a translator has to handle in the process of translating. If translation studies focus merely on the theme and rheme of the clause level, not on the progression of themes and rhemes in the process of clauses' developing into a text, it is largely the same as treating clause or sentence as the unit of translation, which is not supposed to be workable in both the practice of textual translation and the text-oriented translation studies. Therefore, we will probe into textual translation from the perspective of thematic progression.

4.3.2.1 Theoretical speculations

Thematic progression, as a linguistic term, is firstly proposed by Czech linguist Danes, which he defines as "the choice and ordering of utterance themes, their mutual concatenation and hierarchy, as well as their relationship to hyper-themes of the superior text units (such as the paragraph, chapter ...), to the whole text, and to the situation."(Danes, 1974:114) Moreover, "thematic progression exhibits the framework of textual structure." (Huang, 1988:80) Although there are various types and genres of texts, and the connections between themes and rhemes vary from text to text, thematic progression in a text still has certain patterns to follow. Scholars at home and abroad have summarized their respective kinds of TP patterns on the basis of their investigations on textual structure in English as well as other languages. Danes (1974:118-119) firstly put forward five common kinds of TP patterns, and from then up to the present, the frequently-mentioned classifications of TP patterns proposed in succession by researchers are as follows: four types put forward by Xu (1982:3-4); seven types by Huang (1985:34-35); six types by Huang (1988:81-85); three types by Hu (1994:144-145); and four types by Zhu (1995:7). Generally speaking, the connections between themes and rhemes of clauses in a piece of text move forward in line with one of the above-mentioned patterns or some mixed patterns.

TP patterns are the forms of arranging the linguistic materials in a text, and they are an important means in fulfilling the textual functions, for they are of help not only to writers in producing their texts but also to translators in interpreting the original texts. TP is an important information structure of a text, and it serves as an important means to maintain cohesion and coherence and to control the flow of information in the text because "it links up information in the text in a good order and leads to smooth transition from a clause to the next one." (Wang, 2000:35) Every text can be considered as a sequence of themes, presented in the form of mutual connections and gradual progression of themes, and "with the progression of themes in the clauses, the text unfolds itself gradually till it forms a whole one capable of expressing some complete meaning." (Zhu et al., 2001:102-103) TP patterns exhibit the structural framework and overall orientation of a text and reflect the author's methods and intentions of generating the text, so they deserve our special attention in textual translation.

Specific TP patterns chosen by an author to organize a text demonstrate his communicative intentions, so they serve as an important reference for a translator in producing the target text, and he must pay close attention to them and try to reproduce them in the translated text, especially "when the TP patterns in the source text pose an explicit rhetorical purpose, the translator must reproduce them to the best of his ability, and even if it is really impossible to do so, the overall textual effect must be reproduced in the target text." (Liu, 2006:310) Baker (2000:125) points out that "it is necessary to take account of thematic structure and to maintain a coherent point of view in any act of communication." Fawcett (2007:89) also claims that "because thematic breakdown can lead to incoherence, thematic structure does require attention."

Indeed, if TP patterns in the source text are disrupted in the translating process, there will appear awkward flow of information first and then incoherent semantic connections. However, it is not sufficient to merely take thematic progression into account, because cohesion of themes and rhemes demonstrated by TP are the surface connections of a text, and the deep connections in a text lie in its inner semantic coherence. "Cohesion is the network of surface relations which link words and expressions to other words and expressions in a text, and coherence is the network of conceptual relations which underlie the surface text." (Baker, 2000:218) Therefore, the surface cohesion achieved through TP should be combined with deep semantic coherence in the translated text, since translating is a process of transferring between two languages on the basis of semantic meaning.

In principle, the easiest and most effective way of maintaining the textual structure of the source text is to preserve its TP patterns in the target text. Moreover, the target text should best be consistent with the original text in this respect. This surely does not mean that we should imitate the TP patterns in the source text at the cost of giving up semantic coherence of the target text. TP patterns should be preserved without distorting the target text, so it is misleading to suggest that the TP patterns in the original text must be preserved at all costs.

Because English belongs to the Indo-European language family whereas Chinese belongs to the Sino-Tibetan language family, either of them has its distinctive syntactic structures and ways of expression, which will, to some extent, exert influence on the preservation of TP patterns in translation. In this case, it is advisable to adjust TP patterns in the original text or even to re-construct its own TP patterns in the target text in conformity with norms of the target language. "If the thematic patterning of the original cannot be reproduced naturally in the target language, then you will have to abandon it. If you do, you must ensure that your target version has its own method of development and maintains a sense of continuity in its own right." (Baker, 2000:128) That is to say, when it is impossible to keep TP patterns in the original text, the target text should have its own TP patterns on the premise of not destroying textual structure of the source text, in order to compensate for the loss of giving up TP patterns of the source text and achieve the same textual effect in an alternative way. At the same time, the target text should maintain coherence, transmit the original information maximally, comply with the linguistic norms of the target language, and ensure a natural and fluent reading effect. To sum up, a translated text should have such one characteristic of orderly-connected themes and rhemes, smooth flow of information and semantic coherence. Meanwhile, it should yield the same communicative effect and textual purpose as those of the original text.

What deserves our special attention is whether the same TP patterns that are continuously employed in a specific text will have a direct impact on its textual structure or not. If one pattern of TP appears repeatedly in a specific text or paragraph, the structure of the text or paragraph will be clear and easy to follow. Otherwise, frequent change of TP patterns in a certain text can often result in a disorganized textual structure. As a matter of fact, various types of TP patterns are often mixed in a certain text or paragraph due to the author's need to express complicated events or ideas. The most important thing is that the change of TP patterns must serve a specific textual purpose (for example, as a way of introducing a new topic or switching to another topic) and should not cause disorder of textual structure. This is an important principle to bear in mind when a translator deals with transference of TP patterns in the translating process.

4.3.2.2 Case studies

I. Case studies of preserving TP patterns of the source text

Studies have shown that in general, translators have maintained the TP patterns of the source text in the target text, because "generally speaking, the translators always tend to imitate TP patterns of the original text consciously or unconsciously in the English-Chinese translation practice." (Liu, 2006:310) As a matter of fact, the TP patterns of the source text can basically be preserved in the target text. The preservation of the TP patterns of the source text in translation will be discussed through a few examples (Note: theme and rheme are divided by / in the examples of this book).

(13a) Studies/ serve for delight, for ornament and, for ability. Their chief use for delight/ is in privateness; for ornament,/ is in discourse; and for ability,/ is in the judgment and disposition of business. (from Francis Bacon's *Of Studies*)

(13b) 读书 / 足以怡情，足以博彩，足以长才。其怡情也，/ 最见于独处幽居之时；其博彩也，/ 最见于高谈阔论之中；其长才也，/ 最见于

处世判事之际。（from《论读书》translated by Wang Zuoliang）

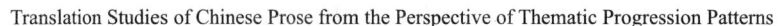

The pattern of thematic progression in Example(13) is a typical TP with a split rheme. The first clause is composed of a theme (Studies) and a rheme (serve for delight; for ornament; for ability) with three information points; In the second sentence, which is made up of three clauses, the three points of information in the rheme of the preceding clause serve as given information (i.e. theme), leading to another three theme-rheme structures. Here, the translator preserves the TP pattern of the source text and reproduces the information structure of the original text.

(14a) 杭州 / 是中国著名的六大古都之一，已有两千多年的历史。杭州 / 不仅以自然美景闻名于世，而且有着传统文化的魅力。/ 不仅有历代文人墨客的题咏，而且有美味佳肴和漂亮的工艺品。（from Sun Wanbiao et al., 2011: 271）

(14b) One of China's six ancient capital cities,/ Hangzhou has a history of more than 2,000 years. It / is famous not only for its natural beauty but also for its cultural traditions. Apart from a large number of poems and inscriptions in its praise left behind by scholars and men of letters through the centuries,/ it also boasts delicious food and pretty handicrafts. (ibid: 277-278)

The pattern of thematic progression in Example(14) is a typical TP with a constant theme. The themes of all clauses in Example(14) are the same, but their rhemes are different. The whole text develops and unfolds itself step by step around the theme of "Hangzhou" and describes it from different angles. The author here has clear communicative intentions (i.e. recommending and publicizing Hangzhou), so the translator should try to reproduce the TP pattern of the original text. However, the pattern of thematic progression in the target text is rather chaotic, which fails to highlight the same theme of "Hangzhou" of the whole text, and thus fails to reproduce the same textual structure and communicative intentions of the source text. We can modify the above translation as below:

(14c) Hangzhou/ is one of China's six ancient capital cities with a history of more than 2,000 years. It/ is famous not only for its natural beauty but also for its cultural traditions. It/ also boasts delicious food and pretty handicrafts as well as a large number of poems and inscriptions in its praise left behind by scholars and men of letters through the centuries.

Comparing this target text with the source text, we can discover that, as far as TP with a constant theme is concerned, English texts often realize the inter-connections of themes of each clause with the help of the reference of pronouns or the use of definite articles, whereas Chinese texts usually emphasize semantic coherence and tend to avoid the repetition of pronouns. After the first theme appears, it is often omitted in subsequent clauses.

II. Case studies of reconstructing TP patterns in the target text

In principle, the easiest way to retain the information structure of the original text in translation is to preserve the TP patterns of the original text. However, Nida & Taber (2004:3-4) point out that "... each language possesses certain distinctive characteristics which give it a special character, ... Rather than force the formal structure of one language upon another, the effective translator is quite prepared to make any and all formal changes necessary to reproduce the message in the distinctive structural forms of the receptor language." Therefore, in view of the differences between English and Chinese, if the TP patterns of the original text cannot be preserved in translation, TP patterns of the target text should be appropriately adjusted on the premise of conforming to the target language norms. Here are a few examples:

(15a) There is no more difference,/ but there is just the same kind of difference, between the mental operations of a man of science and those of an ordinary person as there is between the operations and methods of a baker or of a butcher who weighs out his goods in common scales and the operations of a chemist who performs a difficult and complex analysis by means of his balance and finely graduated weights. (T. H. Huxley from Lian Shuneng (1993: 58)

(15b) 科学家的思维活动和普通人的思维活动之间 / 存在着差别，这种差别 / 就跟一个面包师或者卖肉者和一个化验师在操作方法上的差别一样。前者 / 用普通的秤称东西的重量，而后者 / 则用天平和精密砝码进行艰难复杂的分析。其差别 / 不过如此而已。（ibid: 58）

Due to the hypotactic feature of English, various formal means are often employed to link words or clauses and to create a sentence or even a text, thus explicit cohesion, complete sentences and syntactic structure are highly stressed in English texts. On the contrary, the paratactic feature of Chinese enables us to create a text with little or no use of formal cohesive devices, hence implicit coherence, as well as the logical order of things or events are highlighted in Chinese texts. This kind of differences in syntactic patterns between English and Chinese will be reflected in the cohesion of themes and rhemes in a text. Therefore, in English-Chinese translation, it is often necessary to analyze the sentence structure first and then to figure out its functions and meanings, and make corresponding adjustments when necessary. Only in this way can the translators finally produce a desirable target text. In the above example, the translator is fully conscious of the differences between hypotaxis and parataxis of the two languages. Therefore, instead of sticking to the original TP pattern of the source text, he firstly divides the sentences of the original text according to their grammatical relationships, and then reorganizes the semantic contents of the original text in accordance with the logical order of things. By doing so, the translator constructs a different pattern of thematic progression and reproduces the information structure of the source text.

(16a) 大自然的鬼斧神工，/ 造就了长江三峡绝妙的奇景。气势雄伟的瞿塘峡，逶迤曲折的巫峡，礁石纵横的西陵峡，/ 无不风姿绰约，光彩照人；深藏其间的小三峡，/ 更是曲水通幽，楚楚动人，山翠，水清，峰奇，瀑飞，倾倒了天下多少游人。（from Qiao Ping et al., 2002: 190）

(16b) The Yangtze River/ boasts of the fascinating Three Gorges created by Mother Nature in all her glory. The Three Gorges/ consist of grandiose Qutang Gorge, meandering Wu Gorge and heavily-shoaled Xiling Gorge, all saturated in splendid colors. Tucked away among these/ are three little gorges. All of them/ form a veritable wonderland of clear water with plunging waterfalls and velvety hillsides, often rising to fantastic peaks — beckoning travelers from afar. (ibid: 191)

Since English is a subject-prominent language, while Chinese is a topic-prominent language, and one important feature of topic in the Chinese language is that "once an element is announced as topic, this element may be omitted altogether in subsequent clauses, hence the proliferation of subjectless clauses in languages such as Chinese." (Baker, 2000:142) Therefore, as long as there is a topic for a text or paragraph in Chinese, all kinds of relevant information can be organized and developed around this topic, whereas in English, the information of a text or paragraph is usually organized by themes and unfolded step by step, which is the difference between English and Chinese in terms of information layout. In this case, if the TP patterns of the source text are directly copied in Chinese-English translation, it is highly possible to disrupt the information structure and result in a loose textual structure by introducing various information into the theme of each clause in the target text. Consequently, it is often necessary to adjust the patterns of thematic progression so as to construct a clear information structure in the target text. In Example(16), the Chinese text is developed around the topic of "the fascinating Three Gorges". The cohesion and progression between the theme and rheme of each clause is not obvious and the text structure is relatively loose, but the whole text is still coherent in terms of semantic meanings. Therefore, instead of directly imitating the TP pattern of the original text in translation, the translator makes appropriate adjustments according to the characteristics of English texts, and constructs a cohesive and coherent pattern of thematic progression as well as a clear information structure in the target text.

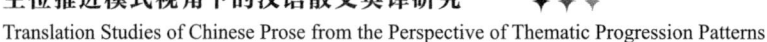

By comparing the English and Chinese texts in the above example, it can be found that the cohesion and semantic coherence of the adjacent clauses in the English text relies heavily on the orderly progression of themes and rhemes, and the theme and rheme of each clause are interconnected mainly through grammatical and lexical devices. By doing so, the meanings and logical relations of the whole text can be effectively expressed, and the explicit connections and textual structure can be shown clearly. However, the interconnections between theme and rheme in Chinese texts is sometimes not as obvious as those in English texts. The cohesion of themes and rhemes in the neighboring sentences is hardly realized by formal cohesive devices. The logical relations of the Chinese texts mainly depend on the semantic meanings of the clauses of the entire text, which is characteristic of implicit coherence. This phenomenon is caused by the linguistic differences between English and Chinese, which deserves much attention in the process of English-Chinese translation.

In translation studies and translation practice, the text should be viewed as a whole. The theme and rheme of each clause in a text are inter-connected with each other, and form the final text through their gradual and orderly progression, which reflect the author's writing methods and communicative intentions. In this sense, the patterns of thematic progression can serve as an important reference for the translator in constructing the target text. As a result, TP patterns in the original text should be preserved to the maximum in the translation. If it is really difficult to keep them directly because of the disparities between different languages, the translator ought to construct properly its own TP patterns in the target text to recreate both textual structure and overall textual effect of the source text. In the actual translation practice, when and how the translator will preserve the TP patterns of the original text or reconstruct the TP patterns in the target text, and whether it will be influenced by the genre of the source text, is worthy of further research.

Chapter 5

Research Design

Specific patterns of thematic progression are an important means in fulfilling the textual functions, so they serve as an important reference for a translator in interpreting the source text and constructing the target text. From the current results of relevant research, we can discover that the application of TP patterns to text-based translation studies up to the present mostly focuses on theoretical speculations supported by some illustrative examples, such as Liu (2006:309-312) and Li et al. (2008:62-66). However, this kind of research is inadequate and unfavorable for us to observe accurately and describe effectively the phenomena of transference of TP patterns actually occurring in the translation process. We still need to conduct a careful and detailed description of the transference of TP patterns in the actual textual translation. Based on the adequate observation analysis, we can describe the various transference and summarize the laws of the transference of TP patterns in textual translation and explain the phenomena from the theoretical perspective.

5.1 Research Questions

Because specific TP patterns chosen on purpose by an author to organize a certain text demonstrate the author's method of planning the text as well as his communicative intentions, they therefore serve as an important factor for consideration in textual translation and an important reference for a translator in constructing the target text. The following research questions are asked:

1) In the existing translated texts, to what extent does a translator stick to the TP patterns found in the source text?

2) In the cases of not preserving them, how does the translator transfer TP patterns of the source text?

3) Do there exist some laws of the transference of TP patterns in Chinese-English translation?

4) Why do the changes of TP patterns occur in Chinese-English translation?

5) What are the conditioning factors that constrain the choices made by the translator?

5.2 Research Hypotheses

Since TP patterns serve as an important textual structure as well as an important means to achieve cohesion and coherence of text, and they reflect the author's communicative intentions and methods of arranging clauses and constructing texts, in theory, a translator should try his best to preserve TP patterns of the source texts. However, the differences between different languages, especially in syntactic structures and ways of expression, will to a certain degree have an impact on maintaining TP patterns in translation. Baker (2000:128) claims that "If the thematic patterning of the original cannot be reproduced naturally in the target language, then you will have to abandon it. If you do, you must ensure that your target version has its own method of development and maintains a sense of continuity in its own right." Therefore, it is postulated that in the great majority of cases, TP patterns in the source text can be preserved in the target text, and meanwhile, due to the differences between Chinese and English, the remaining minority of cases may be adjusted on the grounds of norms of the target text. In addition, the choices of preserving or adjusting TP patterns in Chinese-English translation can be explained to some extent.

5.3 Data Collection

The materials used for the present research are taken from the book entitled *Selected Modern Chinese Prose Writings* (volume 2) rendered into English by Zhang Peiji, with both Chinese texts and their English versions. Because the original Chinese texts are all famous works produced by well-known modern Chinese writers, they serve as significant materials for a comparison between Chinese and English. 15 source texts and their corresponding translated texts are chosen at random from all the 45 texts contained in the book as the object of study. The 15 selected source texts are prose written in the years from 1921 to 1942 by 11 famous modern Chinese writers, and there are 152 paragraphs and about 15,000 Chinese characters in total. After selecting the corpus of original texts as well as their translated versions, we first determine the theme and rheme of each clause in the texts, and then determine the patterns of theme progression in the texts at a higher level (mainly sentence groups). After making such preparations, we can observe and describe the transference of TP patterns in the texts in a detailed way and analyze them on the basis of statistical data.

5.4 Research Methods

Qualitative approach and quantitative approach are adopted jointly in the present research. After establishing definitions of "theme" and "thematic progression", the selected materials are analyzed according to these two definitions, firstly identifying the theme and rheme of each clause in all the materials on the basis of clause, secondly identifying various TP patterns based on sentence group, thirdly observing and describing the distribution frequency of TP patterns in the source texts and target texts as well as the transference of TP patterns from the source texts to the target texts, and finally conducting statistical analysis of them.

On one hand, only when there are at least two or more clauses can their themes and rhemes form thematic progression by connecting with each other. Therefore, a certain TP pattern formed by those two or more clauses is taken as the unit of one sentence group, on the basis of which the transference of TP patterns in textual translation is investigated one by one. On the other hand, in a text, the unit capable of expressing a certain complete meaning is usually the paragraph, which often serves as a translator's focus of attention in the translating process, and which is generally treated as the unit of textual translation used to examine a translator's strategies in text-oriented translation studies, so paragraph is taken as the unit to investigate the translator's strategies adopted in transferring TP patterns. In most cases, a paragraph contains more than one sentence group, each having one TP pattern. In this sense, a paragraph is actually the organic combination of more than one TP pattern. Therefore, it is not only necessary but also useful to investigate the transference of TP patterns both at the level of paragraph and at the level of sentence group.

5.5 Research Feasibility

This research is possible for the following reasons. Firstly, issues of theme and thematic progression have already been explored widely at home and abroad, and mature theories in this field are available at present, which can serve as solid foundation on the basis of which our research are conducted. Secondly, the selected materials used for this study are significant for a comparison between two different languages, because the original Chinese texts are all famous works produced by well-known modern Chinese writers, with their English versions rendered by an experienced and fruitful translator. Thirdly, probing into the laws of transference in textual translation through observing, describing and explaining translational phenomena occurring in the translated texts, as this research does, measures up to the requirements of translation studies as an empirical discipline and at the same time accords with the worldwide trend of translation studies.

Chapter 6

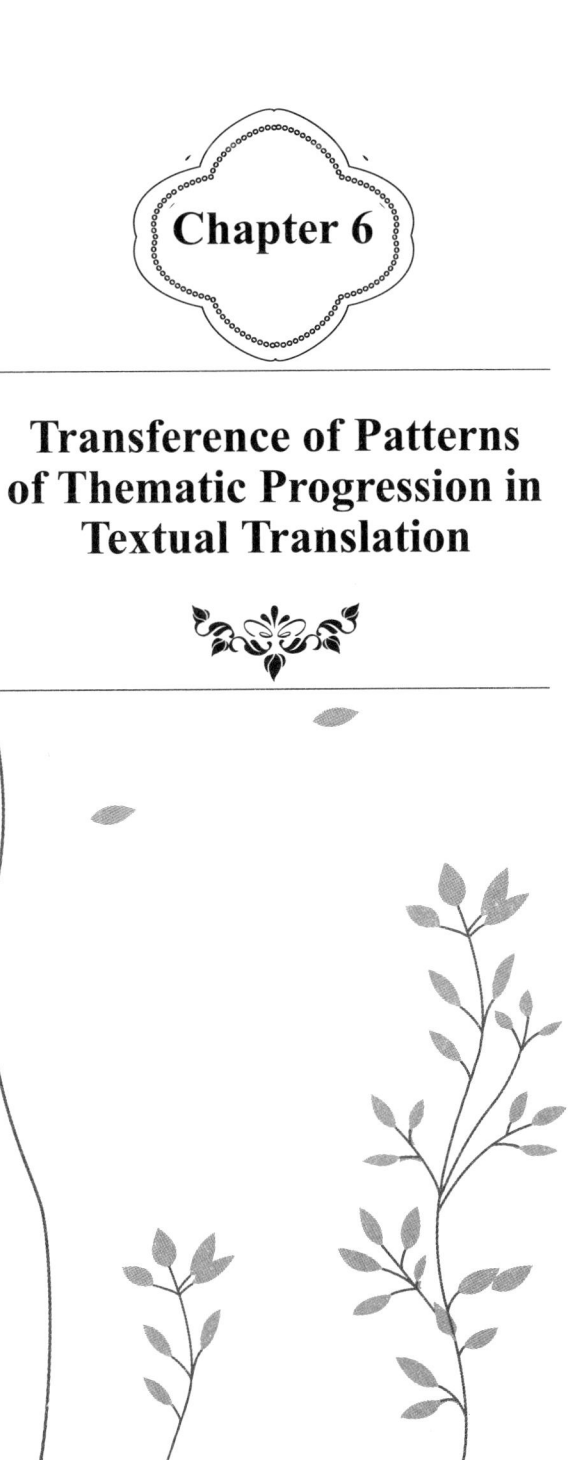

Transference of Patterns of Thematic Progression in Textual Translation

The concept of "thematic progression" is initially put forward by Czech linguist F. Danes (1974:114). Although there are various types and genres of texts, and the connections between themes and rhemes vary from text to text, TP in a text still has certain patterns to follow. Scholars at home and abroad have summarized their respective kinds of TP patterns on the basis of their investigations on textual structure in English as well as other languages. Danes (1974:118-119) firstly put forward five common kinds of TP patterns, and from then up to the present, the frequently-mentioned classifications of TP patterns proposed in succession by researchers are as follows: four types put forward by Xu (1982:3-4); seven types by Huang (1985:34-35); six types by Huang (1988:81-85); three types by Hu (1994:144-145); and four types by Zhu (1995:7). However, the above-mentioned classifications are not sufficient in the process of observing the actual texts, so we intend to re-classify the patterns of thematic progression based on our observation of the actual texts and then make a statistical analysis of them.

6.1 Data Processing

Theme is an important concept in Systemic Functional Grammar. "Theme is the starting-point for the message; it is the ground from which the clause is taking off." (Halliday, 2000:38) Once the Theme is identified, all the rest of the clause is simply labeled the Rheme. Halliday (2000:38) hold that "As a general guide, the Theme can be identified as that element which comes in first position in the clause. We have already indicated that this is not how the category of Theme is defined. The definition is functional, …" (emphasis original) At the same time, Halliday (2000:38) points out that "First position in the clause is not what defines the Theme; it is the means whereby the function of Theme is realized, in the grammar of English." (emphasis original) Jiang (2008:137-146) reviews the evolution of the notion of theme in Systemic Functional Grammar through a detailed examination of the definitions given by Halliday in the past decades or so, and then he claims that firstly, theme and given information are two different notions, although they are often realized by the same element in unmarked situations, and that secondly, theme has been kept apart from what the message is about, i.e. the notion of aboutness, and that thirdly, it's not appropriate to simply equate theme with the initial position of a clause. It seems to us that it is more defendable to stick to the functional notion of theme, that is, to define theme as "the starting-point for the message" in a clause, and to make a clear distinction between the functional notion of theme and the formal notion of theme as "the initial element of a clause". The element which is put at the initial position of a clause is not necessarily the theme, so we should "distinguish between elements which always come initially in a clause and those placed there as a thematic choice." (Jiang, 2008:144) Adhering to this principle is of much significance to guide our identification of themes of clauses in the data.

6.1.1 Data Annotation for Statistics

After collecting the language data for research, we firstly distinguish between theme and rheme of each clause in both the source texts and the target texts, and then move from the clause level upward to the text level and identify the TP patterns in all the texts, and finally observe the transference of

TP patterns from the original Chinese texts to the translated English texts and conduct descriptions as well as statistical analysis of them.

Generally speaking, in data processing we follow Halliday's (2000) practice in identifying the themes of English clauses, and refers to Fang et al. (1995) and Zheng (2000) in analyzing themes and rhemes in Chinese clauses. There are still some special cases in theme analysis that need to be made clear here.

Firstly, there is the issue of theme analysis in the so-called "Enhanced Theme Construction" (ETC) in English. ETC makes use of thematic build-up (also called thematic trigger) to enhance the element that follows closely after it, thus makes the element become enhanced theme, namely, theme enhanced through syntactic structure. "According to Cardiff Grammar, there are three kinds of ETCs in English." (Huang, 1996:66) The first type is experiential ETC, which is termed as cleft sentence in traditional grammar. The second type is evaluative ETC, which is traditionally called extraposed construction. The third type is existential ETC, which is actually "there-be" sentence in traditional grammar. Now it will be shown how to deal with theme analysis in these three types of ETC through specific examples. T and R stand for Theme and Rheme respectively in all the examples listed in this paper. The page numbers appearing in all the examples refer to the page numbers of the book entitled *Selected Modern Chinese Prose Writings* (volume 2).

6.1.1.1 Experiential Enhanced Theme Construction

The first type is experiential ETC, which is termed as cleft sentence in traditional grammar.

(17) It is also due to this "gradualness" (T) that one is able to reconcile himself to his reduced circumstances (R). (p155)

As to Example(17), Halliday (2000:58) and Thompson (2000:128) both term it as "predicated theme" construction. According to their practice, "It is also due to this 'gradualness'" here acts as the theme of this clause with the remainder as the rheme. However, Huang's (1996:47) opinion is quite different from that. He argues that clauses of this kind should be regarded as experiential ETC, and in the light of his approach, "It is" here acts as thematic build-up, "also due to this 'gradualness'" alone serves as enhanced theme, and the rest of this clause is rheme. Huang's approach is adopted in dealing with such clauses in data processing.

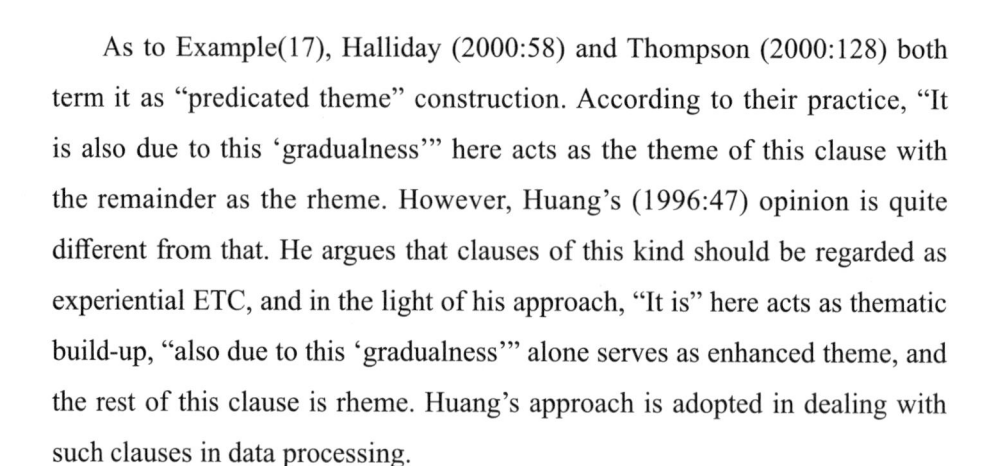

6.1.1.2 Evaluative Enhanced Theme Construction

The second type is evaluative ETC, which is traditionally called extraposed construction.

(18) It is evident (T) that life is sustained by "gradualness" (R). (p155)

With regard to Example(18), according to Halliday's (2000:60-61) practice, "It" is the theme and the remainder is rheme. Thompson (2000:129) label clauses such as this one "thematiced comment" construction, and according to his operation, "It is evident" here assumes the role of theme and the rest of the clause is rheme. Miao (2007:54) argues that clauses of this type should be considered as evaluative ETC, and in accordance with his practice, "It is" here acts as thematic build-up and "evident" plays the part of enhanced theme with the rest being rheme of the clause. Miao's practice is followed in handling such clauses.

6.1.1.3 Existential Enhanced Theme Construction

The third type is existential ETC, which is actually "there-be" sentence in traditional grammar.

(19) There was a farmer (T) who would jump over a ditch holding a calf in his arms on his way to work in the fields every morning and also on his way

back home every evening (R). (p157)

With respect to Example(19), based on Halliday's (2000:44) analysis, "There" is the theme and the rest of the clause is rheme. However, Thompson (2000:138) argues that the existential "there" here "does not fulfill the thematic criterion of expressing experiential meaning", because "the Theme always contains one, and only one, of these experiential elements (either participant, circumstance, or process)." (Halliday, 2000:52) So he claims that "There was" should be identified as the theme of the clause here because they work together to express an existential process, and the remainder is recognized as rheme. Zhang (1998:39-40) claims that clauses such as this one should be treated as existential ETC, and that "there" here cannot measure up to the requirements of theme. Based on his analysis, in this clause "There was" assumes the role of thematic trigger, "a farmer" serves as enhanced theme, and the remainder is rheme. Zhang's operation is adopted in dealing with clauses of this type in data analysis.

Secondly, there is the issue of theme analysis with preposed attributives appearing before the subject theme of a clause in English. Halliday (2000) hasn't discussed this kind of issues in theme analysis, so we turn to Thompson (2000:140-141) for reference when coming across clauses of this kind, that is, to treat the preposed attributives as part of the theme, because "it is expressed as structurally dependent, tethered to the following nominal group, and therefore the nominal group can be taken as forming the real starting-point of the clause." (Thompson, 2000:141) Therefore, the theme of Example(20) is "Young and light-hearted, they", with the rest of this clause being the rheme.

(20) Young and light-hearted, they (T) were indeed basking in the embrace of the god of happiness (R). (p90)

Thirdly, there is the issue of how to identify the theme in a sentence with no subject, which is of frequent occurrence in Chinese. Look at the example(21).

(21a) (T) 真是一个令人不平、令人流泪的情景 (R)。(p80)

(21b) The tragic spectacle (T) is such as to arouse great indignation and draw tears of sympathy (R)! (p82)

This is a typical subjectless clause in the Chinese language, which is treated in our data processing as a clause that has rheme alone with its theme being omitted. Such clauses are all rendered into English in the complete form of a clause, because the subject is indispensable for any sentence according to the norms of the English language.

6.1.2 Identification of TP Patterns

After identifying theme and rheme of each clause in the source texts and target texts, we enter into the level of text to identify the TP patterns in the texts on the basis of sentence group. We adopt the notion of "thematic progression" defined by Danes and find out the following 14 kinds of TP patterns (each with both Chinese and English illustrative examples given below) based on our observations of textual structures in all the selected Chinese and English texts, with the previous classifications of TP patterns proposed by various scholars as the frame of reference.

6.1.2.1 TP with a constant theme

A series of clauses have the same theme but different rhemes, and these rhemes develop around the same theme from different angles.

(22) 它 (T_1) 望着我狂吠 (R_1)，它 (T_2) 张大嘴 (R_2)，它 (T_3) 做出要扑过来的样子 (R_3)。但是它 (T_4) 并不朝着我前进一步 (R_4)。(p176)

(23) First, I (T_1) keep an earnest attitude towards life (R_1). I (T_2) love

orderliness, discipline and cleanliness (R_2). I (T_3) hate to see or hear of things absurd, undisciplined or slack (R_3). (p53)

In the Chinese Example(22), the clauses connect and move forward with the same theme "它". In the English Example(23), the clauses connect and progress with the constant theme "I".

6.1.2.2 TP with a continuous rheme

A series of clauses have the same rheme but different themes, and these themes are all concentrated on the same rheme.

(24) 使人生圆滑进行的微妙的要素 (T_1)，莫如"渐"(R_1)；造物主骗人的手段 (T_2)，也莫如"渐"(R_2)。(p152)

(25) Innumerable poets (T_1) have sung their praises of the window (R_1), innumerable singers (T_2) have extolled it (R_2), innumerable lovers (T_3) have fixed their dreamy eyes on it (R_3). (p259)

In the Chinese Example(24), the clauses move forward through the same rheme "莫如渐". In the English Example(25), the clauses progress with the continuous rheme "the window", which is replaced by the pronoun "it" in the last two clauses.

6.1.2.3 TP with derived themes

In a set of clauses, the themes of other clauses are derived from the theme of the first clause.

(26) 并排的五六个山峰 (T_1)，差不多高低 (R_1)，就只最西的一峰 (T_2) 戴着一簇房子 (R_2)，其余的 (T_3) 仅只有树 (R_3)；中间最大的一峰 (T_4) 竟还有濯濯地一大块，像是癞子头上的疮疤 (R_4)。(p161)

(27) The five or six peaks forming the front row (T_1) were about the same height (R_1). The westernmost one (T_2) had on top a cluster of houses (R_2) while the rest (T_3) were topped by nothing but trees (R_3). The highest one in the middle (T_4) had on it a large piece of barren land, like the scar on a favus-

infected human head (R_4). (p163)

In the Examples(26) and (27), the themes of the last three clauses are derived from the theme of the first clause in both cases, namely, "并排的五六个山峰" and "The five or six peaks forming the front row".

6.1.2.4 TP with a split rheme

In a set of clauses, the rheme of the first clause splits into several semantic elements to serve as themes of the subsequent clauses.

(28) 从北平来的人 (T_1) 往往说在上海这地方怎么"呆"得住 (R_1)。一切 (T_2) 都这样紧张 (R_2)。空气 (T_3) 是这样龌龊 (R_3)。走出去 (T_4) 很难得看见树木 (R_4)。(p27)

(29) Let me (T_1) begin with my family background (R_1). My father (T_2) was a high-ranking naval officer (R_2). He (T_3) was very healthy and strong (R_3) and I (T_4) do not remember ever to have found him confined to bed by sickness (R_4). My grandfather, also very healthy and strong (T_5), died without illness at the age of 86 (R_5). My mother (T_6), however, was very thin and weak, often suffering from headaches and blood-spitting — an illness I was once also liable to (R_6). (p49)

In the Chinese Example(28), part of the rheme of the first clause, namely, "上海这地方", splits into three semantic elements to act as themes of the following three clauses. In the English Example(29), "my family background", part of the rheme of the first clause, splits into several semantic elements to serve as themes of the subsequent clauses.

6.1.2.5 Linear TP

In a series of clauses, the rheme of the preceding clause becomes the theme of the following clause, and this theme introduces a new rheme.

(30) 巨富的纨绔子弟 (T_1) 因屡次破产而"渐渐"荡尽其家产，变为贫者 (R_1); 贫者 (T_2) 只得做雇工 (R_2)，雇工 (T_3) 往往变为奴隶 (R_3)，奴隶 (T_4)

容易变为无赖 (R_4)，无赖 (T_5) 与乞丐相去甚近 (R_5)，乞丐 (T_6) 不妨做偷儿 (R_6)……(p152)

(31) People (T_1) are generally inclined to cherish the memory of their childhood (R_1). Be it happy or sad (T_2), it is always regarded as the most significant part of one's life (R_2). (p49)

In the Chinese Example(30), part of R_1 "贫者" becomes T_2 and the same relation between the rheme of the preceding clause and the theme of the following clause continues till the last clause, which forms a linear thematic progression. In the English Example(31), part of R_1 "their childhood" turns into part of T_2 "it", hence a linear thematic progression.

6.1.2.6 Crisscrossed TP

In a series of clauses, the theme of the preceding clause grows into the rheme of the following clause.

(32) 城门低暗的洞口 (T_1) 正熙熙攘攘地过着商贾路人 (R_1)，一个个 (T_2) 直愣着呆呆的眼睛 (R_2)，"莫谈国事"的唯一社会教育 (T_3) 使他们的嘴都严严封闭着 (R_3)。(p227)

(33) "Time" (T_1) is the essence of "gradualness" (R_1). Ordinary people (T_2) have only a superficial understanding of time (R_2). (p157-158)

In the Chinese Example(32), T_2 "一个个" grows into part of R_3 "他们的嘴"，which composes a crisscrossed TP, and it is the same with the English Example(33), in which T_1 "Time" becomes part of R_2 "time".

6.1.2.7 TP with two alternate themes

In a set of clauses, two different themes appear alternately, and their respective rhemes make corresponding changes.

(34) 西洋人 (T_1) 究竟近乎白痴，什么事都只讲究脚踏实地去做 (R_1)，这样费力气的勾当 (T_2)，我们聪明的中国人，简直连牙齿都要笑掉了 (R_2)。西洋人 (T_3) 什么事都讲究按部就班地慢慢来，从来没有平地登天的捷径

(R_3)，而我们中国人 (T_4) 专门走捷径 (R_4)，而走捷径的第一个法门 (T_5)，就是善吹牛 (R_5)。(p95)

(35) Because of their earnest and down-to-earth approach to work (T_1), Westerners are, in the eyes of Chinese smarties, next door to idiotic (R_1). They (T_2) are being laughed at by Chinese smarties for the tremendous amount of energy they put into their activities (R_2). While Westerners (T_3) go about whatever work they do methodically and patiently, never dreaming of reaching great heights in one stop (R_3), we Chinese (T_4) are always given to seeking a shortcut and regard the ability to boast as the master key to it (R_4). (p97)

In our selected materials, this pattern appears with very low frequency and lacks typicality. Nevertheless, this pattern is still a basic one according to our observations of other texts. In the above Chinese Example(34), two different themes "西洋人" and "我们中国人" can be broadly regarded as appearing alternately, so is the case with the English Example(35) with two alternate themes "Westerners" and "we Chinese".

6.1.2.8 TP with merged theme(s) and rheme(s)

In a series of clauses, the theme(s) and rheme(s) of a clause (some clauses) combine to produce the theme of the following clause.

(36) 甚至在虎圈中，午睡醒来，昂首一呼 (T_1)，还能使猿猴站栗 (R_1)。万兽之王的这种余威 (T_2)，我们也还可以在作了槛内囚徒的虎身上看出来 (R_2)。(p181)

(37) On the eve of the fall of the "Jiang Qing counter-revolutionany clique" (T_1), I used to go to Longhua Park every day for a reading session, seeking shelter from a sea of frosty looks and hostile stares in a world of my own (R_1). That (T_2) will forever remain an unforgettable experience of my life (R_2). (p253)

In the Examples(36) and (),37 T_2 is the semantic combination of T_1 and

R_1, thus both of them form a TP with merged theme and rheme.

6.1.2.9 Intermittent TP (also TP with intervals between)

In a series of clauses, connections exist between themes and rhemes of clauses not adjacent to each other, causing the thematic progression to jump forward with intervals between.

(38) 我 (T_1) 也不能不感谢这个转变 (R_1)！十岁以前的训练 (T_2)，若再继续下去，我就很容易变成一个男性的女人，心理也许就不会健全 (R_2)。因着这个转变 (T_3)，我才渐渐的从父亲身边走到母亲的怀里，而开始我的少女时期了 (R_3)。(p47)

(39) A fall of snow a couple of days before (T_1) had brought to the city dwellers a touch of brightness (R_1), but now (T_2) what an ugly scene reigned (R_2)! The raw wind (T_3) sent the snow on the tiles along the eaves whirling in the air in tiny bits and adroitly making its way down the necks of the pedestrians by way of their collars (R_3). The streets (T_4) had become slushy by exposure to the prankish sun (R_4), and the thawing snow (T_5) was dotted with traces of footsteps (R_5). (p228)

In the Chinese Example(38), the thematic connections exist between T_1 and R_3, as well as between R_1 and T_3, so the thematic progression here jumps forward with intervals between them. In the English Example(39), the thematic connection exists between T_1, R_3 and T_5, which forms an intermittent TP.

6.1.2.10 TP with inserted elements

Some elements, usually a clause or some clauses, that have no obvious connections with themes or rhemes of the other clauses in a piece of text are occasionally inserted into the process of thematic progression.

(40) 我的老师 (T_1) 很爱我，常常教我背些诗句 (R_1)，我 (T_2) 似懂似不懂的有时很能欣赏 (R_2)。比如那"前不见古人，后不见来者，念天地

之悠悠，独怆然而涕下"(T_3)。我独立山头的时候(T_4)，就常常默诵它(R_4)。(p46)

(41) The dark low archway of the city gate (T_1) was thronged with tradesmen and pedestrians passing to and fro, each staring blankly ahead (R_1). Acting on the public warning "No discussing state affairs" (T_2), people had learned to keep their mouths closely shut (R_2). Yes, trouble (T_3) seemed to be brewing (R_3). But they (T_4) knew not the trouble was between whom and whom (R_4). (p229)

In the Chinese Example(40), the third clause, which is an incomplete sentence and has no obvious connection with any theme or rheme of the other clauses, is inserted into the process of thematic progression. In the English Example(41), the thematic progression moves forward with an inserted element, namely, the third clause.

6.1.2.11 TP with no regular pattern

The themes and rhemes of a series of clauses have no regular connections with each other, but they serve the whole text or a certain topic directly.

(42) 同时那北海的红漪清波(T_1)浮现在眼前(R_1)，那些手携情侣的男男女女(T_2)，恐怕也正摇着画桨，指点着眼前清丽秋景，低语款款吧(R_2)！况且又是菊茂蟹肥时候(T_3)，料想长安市上，车水马龙，正不少欢乐的宴聚(R_3)，这漂泊异国，秋思凄凉的我们(T_4)当然是无人想起的(R_4)。(p87)

(43) Was she (T_1) overcome with regret (R_1)? Maybe, but who (T_2) knows (R_2)! How (T_3) the military life had shaped her disposition (R_3)! How rhythmical and plaintive (T_4) the bugle sounded from the barracks at twilight (R_4)! Were tender feelings and soft passions (T_5) exclusive to young girls (R_5)? (p60-61)

In the Examples(42) and (43), it is hard to identify some regular pattern of connections and progression of their themes and rhemes, but these themes and rhemes work together to serve the whole text or a certain topic directly, so the connections between these themes and rhemes are labeled TP with no regular pattern.

6.1.2.12 Framework TP (also TP with a super-theme)

A phrase or clause at a higher level appears first as the super-theme, and a set of clauses at the same lower level follow behind.

(44) 在不知不觉之中 (T_0)，天真烂漫的孩子 (T_1) "渐渐" 变成野心勃勃的青年 (R_1)；慷慨豪侠的青年 (T_2) "渐渐" 变成冷酷的成人 (R_2)；血气旺盛的成人 (T_3) "渐渐" 变成顽固的老头子 (R_3)。(p152)

(45) This (T_0) does not mean, however, that happiness and optimism (T_1) are no good (R_1), healthy wakefulness (T_2) is undesirable (R_2), sweets of life (T_3) are evil (R_3) and hearty laughter (T_4) is vicious (R_4). (p36)

Here T_0 stands for super-theme, which refers to an element appearing at a higher level compared with other elements in a piece of text and acting as a framework under which several clauses develop. In the Chinese Example(44), "在不知不觉之中" here serves as the overall adverbial element of the subsequent three clauses. In the English Example(45), "This" is the subject of the sentence and the following four clauses just function as subordinate objective clauses.

6.1.2.13 Parallel TP (also TP with parallel structures)

A group of three or more clauses have parallel structures, each clause having its own distinct theme and rheme.

(46) 所以心如槁木 (T_1) 不如工愁多感 (R_1)，迷蒙的醒 (T_2) 不如热的梦 (R_2)，一口苦水 (T_3) 胜于一盏白汤 (R_3)，一场痛哭 (T_4) 胜于哀乐两忘 (R_4)。(p33)

(47) Therefore, being sentimental (T_1) is better than apathetic (R_1), having

a warm dream (T_2) is better than becoming a living corpse (R_2), drinking a bitter cup (T_3) is better than a cup of insipid water (R_3), having a good cry (T_4) is better than being insensitive to both sorrow and happiness (R_4). (p36)

In either of the above Chinese Example(46) and English Example(47), the four clauses have the same structure and run parallel, and each clause has its distinct theme and rheme, which has no connection with the themes or rhemes of the other clauses, so this kind of thematic progression is termed as parallel TP.

6.1.2.14 TP with zero / implicit theme

In a series of clauses, after the theme of the first clause appears, the themes of the subsequent clauses are omitted.

(48) 它 (T_1) 展着笔直的翅膀 (R_1)，(T_2) 掠过苍老的树枝 (R_2)，(T_3) 掠过寂静的瓦房 (R_3)，(T_4) 掠过皇家的御湖 (R_4)，(T_5) 环绕灿烂的琉璃瓦 (R_5)，(T_6) 飞着 (R_6)，(T_7) 飞着 (R_7)。(p227)

(49) I (T_1) never played with a doll (R_1), (T_2) never learned how to do needlework (R_2), (T_3) never used cosmetics (R_3), (T_4) never wore colors or flowers (R_4). (p50)

In the Chinese Example(48), the element "它" acts as the theme of all the clauses, but it only appears in the first clause and is omitted in all the following clauses, so there appears implicit theme as well as TP with implicit theme. The same is with the English Example(49). In our selected materials, there is only one instance of this pattern in all the English translated texts and it is due to the impact of its source text. On the contrary, this pattern abounds in the original Chinese texts. The striking difference in this respect results from the distinct linguistic norms of English and Chinese.

Generally speaking, the connections between themes and rhemes of clauses in a piece of text move forward in line with one of the above-mentioned patterns or some mixed patterns. Some points have to be made clear here. Firstly, when a clause employs the theme or rheme of the preceding clause, it does not necessarily copy them word for word, but it usually resorts to part of their semantic contents, or it may develop or change their original semantic contents to some extent. Secondly, these afore-mentioned patterns are merely the basic TP patterns to describe the development of a text. In the practical language use, it happens frequently that several patterns tend to work together in a text in order to express a complicated idea or event. The overall TP patterns in a text are the organic combination of these basic patterns, each pattern playing a certain role in the overall framework of the text.

After identifying various TP patterns occurring in the original and translated texts, the distribution frequency of these patterns in the source texts and the target texts are obtained respectively.

Table 1 Distribution frequency of TP patterns in the original texts

TP pattern	number of occurrences	percentage
TPCT	61	18.3%
LTP	60	18.0%
TPZT	42	12.6%
TPRP	35	10.5%
ITP	27	8.1%
CTP	26	7.8%
TPCR	18	5.4%
TPTR	14	4.2%
FTP	13	3.9%
TPSR	8	2.4%

Continued

TP pattern	number of occurrences	percentage
PTP	5	1.5%
TPDT	4	1.2%
TPIE	3	0.9%
TPAT	1	0.3%
CP	16	4.8%
total	333	100%

Compound pattern here refers to the case in which two or more different TP patterns are used together in a sentence group. (the same below)

Seen from Table 1, those patterns with high frequency of occurrence are the following four patterns, namely, TP with a constant theme, linear TP, TP with zero theme, and TP with no regular pattern, which altogether account for 59.4% of the total occurrences. Among them TP with a constant theme and linear TP occur with the highest frequency in both source texts and target texts, partly because they are the two patterns most extensively used in organizing a text. Compared with the translated texts, the most striking difference lies in the copious instances of TP with zero theme in the original Chinese texts, which is due to the paratactic feature of the Chinese language. The high ratio of TP with no regular pattern occurring in the Chinese texts originates from both traits of Chinese prose writings such as following no set pattern and taking advantage of a scene or an event to give vent to one's feelings in the form of narration interspersed with comments, and the style of writing characteristic of Chinese literati such as having a preference for ornate wording and loading their pages with extensive quotations.

Table 2 Distribution frequency of TP patterns in the translated texts

TP pattern	number of occurrences	percentage
TPCT	83	28.8%
LTP	73	25.3%
CTP	26	9.0%
TPRP	25	8.7%
ITP	22	7.6%
TPCR	19	6.6%
FTP	12	4.2%
TPTR	8	2.8%
TPSR	5	1.7%
TPDT	2	0.7%
TPIE	2	0.7%
PTP	2	0.7%
TPAT	1	0.4%
TPZT	1	0.4%
CP	7	2.4%
total	288	100%

Seen from Table 2, those patterns with high frequency of occurrence are TP with a constant theme and linear TP, which occupy a dominant position in the translated texts by making up 54.1% of the total occurrences. The ratio of these two commonest patterns occurring in the translated texts is higher than that in the source texts, which to a certain degree reflects the tendency for normalization in the translated texts.

In this part we have summarized 14 patterns of thematic progression on the basis of our observations of actual Chinese and English texts and described the frequency distribution of these patterns in the original and translated texts. On this basis, we are able to describe and analyze the transference of TP patterns in Chinese-English textual translation, and then try to discover both the reasons for the transference and the constraints underlying the changes of TP patterns during the translating process.

6.2 Strategies of Transference of TP Patterns (Based on Paragraph)

Observing the transference of TP patterns based on paragraph, three types of strategies adopted by the translator are discovered, namely, preserving TP patterns of the source text, adjusting TP patterns of the source text, and reconstructing TP patterns of the target text.

6.2.1 Statistical Analysis

Distribution of these three different strategies employed by the translator in constructing the target texts is shown in the Table 3.

Table 3 Transference of TP patterns (based on paragraph)

strategy adopted in translation	number of paragraphs	percentage
preserving TP patterns of the ST	38	27.9%
adjusting TP patterns of the ST	71	52.2%
reconstructing TP patterns of the TT	27	19.9%
total	136	100%

The selected materials (original texts) used for this study include 152 paragraphs, among which 16 paragraphs contain only one sentence and thus cannot be analyzed in terms of TP patterns, so the valid materials add up to 136 paragraphs. The translated texts have the same number of paragraphs as the original texts.

If the strategies adopted by the translator to transfer TP patterns in constructing the target texts are investigated on the basis of paragraph, it can be seen from Table 3 that both preserving TP patterns of the source text and reconstructing TP patterns of the target text occur with a low ratio of the total numbers whereas adjusting TP patterns of the source text occurs at a high ratio. The Table 3 shows that from the angle of paragraph-based observation, the result is in disagreement with our hypothesis, as the strategy of keeping TP patterns of the source text actually employed by the translator merely accounts for 27.9%, and in most cases, what the translator does to the TP patterns found in the source texts is to adjust or reconstruct them. Three typical examples from the selected materials in which these three strategies are adopted respectively by the translator are given below.

6.2.2 Preserving TP Patterns in the Source Text

Preserving TP patterns of the source text refers to completely imitating the TP patterns found in the original text in a translator's constructing the target text.

(50a) 她 (T_1) 男装到了十岁 (R_1), 十岁以前 (T_2), 她父亲常常带她去参与那军人娱乐的宴会 (R_2)。朋友们 (T_3) 一见都夸奖说, "好英武的一个小军人！今年几岁了？" (R_3) 父亲 (T_4) 先一面答应着, 临走时才微笑说, "她是我的儿子, 但也是我的女儿。" (R_4) (p57)

(50b) She (T_1) was always dressed like a male child until she was ten (R_1). Before that (T_2), her father would often take her with him when he attended dinner parties arranged for the recreation of servicemen (R_2). Her father's friends (T_3), the moment they saw her, would praise her by saying, "What a heroic little soldier! How old are you now?"(R_3) Her father (T_4) would end up the small talk smilingly with, "She's my son as well as my daughter."(R_4) (p59)

In Example(50), the linear TP formed by R_1 and T_2 as well as the intermittent TP composed by R_2 and T_4 are both preserved directly in the translated text.

6.2.3 Adjusting TP Patterns in the Source Text

Adjusting TP patterns of the source text means changing part of the TP patterns found in the source text while sticking to its basic textual framework in a translator's constructing the target text.

(51a) 唉！这 (T_1) 仅仅是九年后的今天 (R_1)。呀，这短短的九年中 (T_0)，我 (T_2) 走的是崎岖的世路 (R_2)，我 (T_3) 攀缘过陡峭的崖壁 (R_3)，我 (T_4) 由死的绝谷里逃命 (R_4)，使我 (T_5) 尝着忍受由心头淌血的痛苦 (R_5)，命运 (T_6) 要我喝干自己的血汁，如同喝玫瑰酒一般 (R_6)……(p86)

(51b) Oh, nine years (T_1) had quickly passed since then (R_1). During the nine fleeting years (T_0), I (T_2) had trekked on the rugged journey of life, climbed up steep cliffs, and made good my narrow escape from the valley of death (R_2). I (T_3) had experienced the agony of a bleeding heart (R_3). I (T_4) had been forced by destiny to drink up my own blood like I did red wine (R_4) … (p90)

In this instance, the framework TP of the original text (starting from T_0 as the super-theme till the end of this paragraph) is well maintained in the target text. Some adjustments are made under this basic textual framework, namely, the linear TP formed by R_1 and T_0 is changed into the TP with a constant theme composed by T_1 and T_0; the TP with a constant theme formed from T_2 to T_4 is transformed into one clause with T_2 as its theme through the merging of clauses; the crisscrossed TP composed by T_5 and R_6 is changed into the TP with a constant theme formed by T_3 and T_4.

6.2.4 Reconstructing TP Patterns in the Target Text

By "reconstructing TP patterns of the target text" we mean that a translator disrupts the original TP patterns and then builds new TP patterns completely different from those found in the source text when he constructs the target text.

(52a) 飞机 (T_1) 由一个熟悉的方面飞来了 (R_1), 洪大的震响 (T_2) 惊动了当地的居民 (R_2)。他们脸上 (T_3) 各画着一些恐怖的回忆 (R_3)。爬在车辙中玩着泥球的孩子们 (T_4) 也住了手, 仰天望着这只奇怪的蜻蜓, 像是意识出一些严重 (R_4)。及至蜻蜓 (T_5) 为树梢掩住 (R_5), 他们 (T_6) 又重新低下头去玩那肮脏的游戏了 (R_6)。(p227)

(52b) A plane (T_1) appeared out of the blue from a direction only too familiar to the local inhabitants, roaring to the alarm of everybody, on whose face was written memories of some previous horrors (R_1). Kids, who had been crawling about over ruts playing a game of small clay balls (T_2), now stopped to look up at the strange dragonfly in the sky, subconsciously feeling that something ominous was going to happen (R_2). However, they (T_3) soon lowered their heads again to bury themselves in the messy game (R_3) as soon as the dragonfly (T_4) disappeared from view behind the treetops (R_4). (p228)

In the above Example(52), the original TP patterns are thoroughly altered by the translator. The TP with a constant theme formed by T_1 and T_2 together with the linear TP formed by R_2 and T_3 is transformed into one clause with T_1 as its theme via the merging of clauses. The intermittent TP composed by T_4 and T_6 is changed into the TP with a constant theme composed by T_2 and T_3. The linear TP formed by R_4 and T_5 is changed into the intermittent TP formed by R_2 and T_4.

6.3 Transference of TP Patterns (Based on Sentence Group)

When observing the transference of TP patterns based on sentence group, two methods of transferring are discovered, i.e. maintaining the original TP patterns and changing the original TP patterns.

6.3.1 Statistical Analysis

Distribution of these two distinct methods used by the translator in constructing the target texts is shown in the Table 4.

Table 4 Transference of TP patterns (based on sentence group)

method of transferring	number of occurrences	percentage
maintaining the original TP patterns	154	45.6%
changing the original TP patterns	184	54.4%
total	338	100%

If the methods employed by the translator to transfer TP patterns in constructing the target texts are examined on the basis of sentence group, it can be known from Table 4 that the ratio of maintaining the original TP patterns is lower than that of changing the original TP patterns. The Table 4 tells us that from the perspective of sentence-group-based observation, the result of our field survey still runs contrary to our hypothesis, since the method of keeping the original TP patterns actually made use of by the translator makes up 45.6%, which is still of lower frequency than that of changing the original TP patterns. Detailed analysis of each of these two quite different methods of transferring is presented below.

6.3.2 Maintaining the Original TP Patterns

What comes next is the detailed distribution of TP patterns being kept by the translator in constructing the target texts.

Table 5   Distribution of unchanged TP patterns in translation

TP pattern	number of occurrences	percentage
LTP	35	22.7%
TPCT	32	20.8%
ITP	18	11.7%
TPRP	16	10.4%
FTP	12	7.8%
CTP	11	7.1%
TPCR	8	5.2%
TPSR	5	3.3%
TPTR	5	3.3%
TPDT	2	1.3%

Continued

TP pattern	number of occurrences	percentage
TPIE	2	1.3%
PTP	2	1.3%
TPAT	1	0.6%
TPZT	1	0.6%
CP	4	2.6%
total	154	100%

From Table 5 it can be seen clearly that among all the unchanged TP patterns in the translator's constructing the target texts, four patterns occur with a much higher frequency than others, namely, linear TP, TP with a constant theme, intermittent TP and TP with no regular pattern. They account for 65.6% of the total occurrences, which suggests that the probability of these four patterns (especially the former two patterns) being kept in translating from Chinese to English is greater than that of other patterns. Of course, this is no more than a tentative conclusion that remains to be tested by large-scale data. The cases of unchanged TP patterns in Chinese-English textual translation are owing to the common grounds between these two languages, which serve as the basis for translating from one language to another.

6.3.3 Changing the original TP patterns

What follows is the detailed distribution of TP patterns being changed by the translator in constructing the target texts.

Table 6 Distribution of TP patterns in the STs being changed in translation

TP pattern	number of occurrences	percentage
TPZT	41	22.3%
TPCT	29	15.8%
LTP	25	13.6%
TPRP	19	10.3%
CTP	15	8.1%
TPCR	10	5.4%
TPTR	9	4.9%
ITP	9	4.9%
TPSR	3	1.6%
PTP	3	1.6%
TPDT	2	1.1%
TPIE	1	0.5%
FTP	1	0.5%
TPAT	0	0
CP	12	6.5%
OC	5	2.7%
total	184	100%

The cases of one clause are caused by the translator's re-organizing the clauses, including merging the clauses and separating them. The translator's merging (or separating) the clauses of the original texts will lead to the decrease (or increase) of clauses and consequently of TP patterns in the translated texts.

Seen from Table 6, four TP patterns, namely, TP with zero theme, TP with a constant theme, linear TP and TP with no regular pattern, account for

62% of all the TP patterns of the source texts being changed by the translator in constructing the target texts. Among them TP with zero theme occurs most frequently with the number of occurrences being 41, which makes up 22.3% of the total number.

Two causes are found responsible for this phenomenon. The first cause is the paratactic feature of the Chinese language and the consequent characteristics of its syntactic structures and textual structures. In a piece of Chinese text, a topic theme of a clause is often followed by a succession of streamlined clauses with their themes omitted to comment on the topic. This chain of incomplete clauses is normally not subject to the confines of syntax as long as they maintain semantic coherence, which results in the frequent occurrence of TP with zero theme.

The other cause is the hypotactic feature of the English language and the consequent characteristics of its syntactic structures. Much emphasis is laid on the completeness and standardization of sentence-making in English, so those incomplete clauses in Chinese texts are changed into one or some well-formed clauses through the re-structuring of clauses when they are translated into English. Apart from that, the strategies and methods employed by the translator are responsible for the frequent occurrences of the other three patterns, which will be dealt with in later chapters.

Table 7 Distribution of changed TP patterns in the TTs

TP pattern	number of occurrences	percentage
TPCT	51	27.7%
LTP	38	20.7%
CTP	15	8.1%
TPCR	11	6.0%

Continued

TP pattern	number of occurrences	percentage
TPRP	9	4.9%
ITP	4	2.2%
TPTR	3	1.6%
TPDT	0	0
TPSR	0	0
FTP	0	0
TPIE	0	0
PTP	0	0
TPAT	0	0
TPZT	0	0
CP	3	1.6%
OC	50	27.2%
total	184	100%

From Table 7 we can find out two kinds of noticeable figures in the construction of the target texts. Firstly, TP with a constant theme and linear TP, together with the case of one clause, dominate the occurrences by constituting 75.6% of the total occurrences. Secondly, seven types of TP patterns do not appear at all in the construction of the target texts. These two kinds of striking figures imply that the target texts have a tendency for normalization as far as transference of TP patterns is concerned, because the two commonest kinds of TP patterns are used in the target texts much more frequently than in the original texts while those seven types of patterns with low frequency of use are not employed.

Moreover, the frequent occurrences of the case of one clause are caused by the merging of clauses in the process of translating. On one hand, in the original texts there are large numbers of the strings of clauses which are closely connected through their inner meanings and based on a certain topic with subsequent comments. On the other hand, the haphazard use of punctuation characterizes the original texts, which are all prose texts written in a special period. As a result, the translator adopts the method of merging the clauses frequently, which contributes to produce well-arranged translated texts to some extent and results in the drop of the number of clauses in the translated texts as well as the decrease of TP patterns by 45 compared with those in the original texts.

Table 8 Ten types of transference of TP patterns with higher frequency

type of transference (ST → TT)	number of occurrences	percentage
TPZT → TPCT	23	12.5%
TPCT → OC	11	6.0%
TPZT → OC	10	5.4%
TPCT → LTP	10	5.4%
LTP → OC	8	4.2%
LTP → TPCT	6	3.3%
CTP → TPCT	6	3.3%
TPRP → LTP	6	3.3%
TPRP → OC	6	3.3%
TPZT → LTP	6	3.3%
total	92	50%

The results of statistical analysis indicate that the total number of transference of TP patterns in translation is 184, including 66 different types of transference.

Seen from Table 8, the ten types of transference of TP patterns with higher frequency of occurrence are transferring to TP patterns with a constant theme and linear TP and the case of one clause in the translator's constructing the target texts. The total number of transferring to these three cases is 92, accounting for 50% of all the cases of transference, which also proves that there is a tendency for normalization in the target texts in terms of TP patterns, because the two commonest patterns are used more frequently in the target texts. As regards to the frequent occurrence of the case of one clause, it is brought about by the frequent merging of clauses conducted by the translator in the process of translating.

Of all the TP patterns of the source texts being changed by the translator, the ten types of transference with more frequent occurrence are transferring from TP patterns with zero theme, TP with a constant theme, linear TP, TP with no regular pattern and crisscrossed TP. These five cases of transference make up 50% of all the cases of transference. The total number of transference of TP patterns in translation is 184, which involves 66 different types of transference. These ten types of transference of TP patterns account for 50% of the total transference with the number being 92.

So we hold the view that these ten types of transference which occur more frequently can represent to a considerable degree the laws of transference of TP patterns in Chinese-English textual translation. This initial conclusion certainly needs to be tested, modified and enriched in the future on the basis of conducting further empirical study through large-scale data.

6.4 Analysis of the Changes of TP Patterns

Because the TP pattern is the textual layout composed of themes and rhemes of the clauses in a stretch of text, so the changes of TP patterns are directly due to the changes of themes and rhemes at the clause level.

6.4.1 Statistical Analysis

A variety of causes for the changes of TP patterns in translation are offered below.

Table 9   Causes directly responsible for the changes of TP patterns in translation

causes	number of occurrences	percentage
ST topic theme to TT subject theme	31	10.9%
ST implicit theme to TT explicit theme	39	13.7%
ST theme transferred to TT rheme	82	28.8%
clauses re-organized in TT	80	28.0%
other causes	53	18.6%
total	285	100%

Table 9 shows that the first two causes, namely, topic theme in Chinese being transferred to subject theme in English and implicit theme in Chinese being transferred to explicit theme in English, which are caused by the linguistic differences between English and Chinese, occur less frequently and only account for 24.6% of all the causes whereas the next two causes, namely, theme in the source text being transferred to rheme in the target text and clauses being re-organized in the target text, which are caused mostly by the translator's translation strategies and methods, occur with relatively higher frequency and make up 56.8% of the total causes.

This suggests that transference of TP patterns in Chinese-English textual translation are not only subject to the linguistic differences between these two languages, but more frequently under the influence of the translation strategies and methods adopted by a translator. This also explains why the ratio of preserving or maintaining TP patterns is lower than that of adjusting or changing them from our paragraph-based and sentence-group-based observations, and consequently accounts for the inconsistence between our hypotheses and our statistical results, because when we put forward the theoretical hypotheses, we just take into consideration the linguistic differences between two languages, but give little regard to the subjective initiative of a translator and its impact on the translated texts. Typical examples for each of the above-mentioned causes are given below.

6.4.2 Topic Theme in Chinese Being Transferred to Subject Theme in English

Sometimes a topic theme in the original Chinese texts is transferred to a subject theme in the English target texts.

(53a) 提到童年 (T), 总使人有些向往 (R)。(p45)

(53b) People (T) are generally inclined to cherish the memory of their childhood (R). (p49)

In the above Example(53), "提到童年" is the topic theme of the original Chinese clause, but in the translated English clause, it is the element "People", which is the subject theme of the clause, that serves as its theme as well as its subject.

6.4.3 Implicit Theme in Chinese Being Transferred to Explicit Theme in English

Sometimes an implicit theme in the original Chinese texts is transferred to an explicit theme in the English target texts, which can be categorized into two cases.

1. The theme of a Chinese clause is omitted when it employs the same theme of the preceding clause.

(54a) 她 (T_1) 会打走队的鼓 (R_1), (T_2) 会吹召集的喇叭 (R_2), (T_3) 知道毛瑟枪里的机关 (R_3), (T_4) 也会将很大的炮弹旋进炮腔里 (R_4)。(p57)

(54b) She (T_1) learned how to beat the drum for soldiers marching in parade and blow the bugle for the fall-in (R_1). She (T_2) was familiar with the mechanism of a Mauser (R_2). She (T_3) also knew how to feed a big shell into the barrel of a cannon (R_3). (p59)

In Example(54), "她" appears as the theme of the first clause in the Chinese text, and then it is omitted in the following three clauses just because these clauses employ the same element to act as their themes, hence implicit themes. However, in the translated English text, "She" appears three times to serve as the respective explicit themes of the three clauses although the same theme is chosen in these three clauses.

2. The theme of a Chinese clause is omitted when it resorts to (part of) the rheme of the preceding clause.

(55a) 江南的春天 (T_1) 素称多雨 (R_1), (T_2) 一落就是七八天 (R_2)。(p246)

(55b) Spring in the south (T_1) is known to be rainy (R_1). During this season (T_2), it never rains there but it remains wet for seven or eight days on end (R_2). (p247)

In Example(55), as for the second clause in the Chinese text, its theme is omitted because it resorts to part of the rheme of the first clause, and the implicit theme here is "雨". In the translated English text, the theme of the second clause is "During this season", which is an explicit one, although it is different from the implicit theme of the original second clause.

6.4.4 Theme in the Source Text Being Transferred to Rheme in the Target Text

There are occasions when the theme of a clause in the source text is transferred to the rheme of its corresponding clause in the target text.

(56a) 在宁静的环境，悠闲的心情中静静地读书 (T)，是人生中最有味的享受 (R)。(p251)

(56b) It is the greatest joy of life (T) for one to spend his leisure time reading in quiet surroundings (R). (p253)

In Example(56), the element "在宁静的环境，悠闲的心情中静静地读书", which serves as the theme of the original Chinese clause, is translated as "for one to spend his leisure time reading in quiet surroundings" that is put at the position of the rheme of the English clause.

6.4.5 Clauses Being Re-Organized in the Target Text

There are also occasions when clauses in the source text are re-organized in the target text, which generally falls into three types.

6.4.5.1 Clauses Being Merged

(57a) 一群骄傲于幸福的少女们 (T_1)，她们孕育着玫瑰色的希望 (R_1)，当她们将由学校毕业的那一年 (T₂)，曾随了她们德高望重的教师，带着欢乐的心情，渡过日本海来访蓬莱的名胜 (R₂)。在她们登岸的时候 (T₃)，正是暮春三月樱花乱飞的天气 (R₃)。(p86)

(57b) One late spring, when cherry trees were in full bloom (T), a group of young Chinese girls, proud of their happy girlhood and hopeful about the future, merrily crossed the Sea of Japan together with their beloved teacher to visit the scenic spots of Japan in the year when they were about to graduate from school (R). (p89)

In Example(57), the original Chinese text has three closely-connected yet separate clauses, but in the English translated text these three clauses are merged into one clause, with the element "One late spring, when cherry trees were in full bloom," as its theme.

6.4.5.2 Clauses Being Separated

(58a) 井底似的庭院，铅色的水门汀地 (T)，秋虫早已避去唯恐不速了 (R)。(p34)

(58b) The courtyard (T₁) is as still as the bottom of a well (R₁), the cement ground (T₂) is leaden (R₂). Insects (T₃) have long been keeping clear of a place like this (R₃). (p36-37)

In Example(58), the original Chinese text has only one clause, with the element "井底似的庭院，铅色的水门汀地" as its topic theme. However, this clause is separated into three clauses in its English version.

6.4.5.3 Clauses Being Disrupted and Then Re-Organized

(59a) 这几年 (T₁) 投荒到都市 (R₁)，每值淫雨 (T₂)，听着滞涩枯燥的调子，回念故乡景色，觉得连雨声也变了 (R₂)。人事的变迁 (T₃)，更何待说呢 (R₃)！(p246)

(59b) In recent years (T₁), living, as I do, in a big city remote from my old home, I invariably feel homesick listening to the harsh, monotonous drip, drip,

drip of the rain (R_1). O even the sound of rain has changed (T_2), to say nothing of the affairs of human life (R_2)! (p248)

In Example(59), the three clauses in the original Chinese text is disrupted and then re-organized to become two clauses in the English translated text. Added to this change is the fact that the contents of the original themes are somewhat different from those of the themes in the target text.

6.4.6 Other Causes

Detailed sub-classification of "other causes" in Table 9 is presented below.

Table 10 Sub-classification of "other causes" in Table 9

causes	number of occurrences	percentage
other types of thematic adjustments	27	50.9%
different ways of organizing a sentence	15	28.3%
other cases	11	20.8%
total	53	100%

Some points about Table 10 have to be made clear here. Firstly, other types of thematic adjustments can be further classified into six kinds which will be explained below in a detailed way. Secondly, different ways of expressing a sentence include different ways of expressing exclamatory sentences and imperative sentences between Chinese and English, some other ways of expressing Chinese subjectless clauses in English, and the change of sentence pattern, like a declarative sentence in Chinese being changed into an exclamatory sentence in English. Thirdly, other cases here refer to the change of word order in translating as well as some additions and deletions in the translated texts.

Some typical examples are offered to explain the six kinds of thematic adjustments.

1. The translator adds some elements into a clause on the basis of his understanding and makes that element fulfill the role of theme in the translated text.

(60a) 母亲 (T_1) 很早就进去休息 (R_1)，父亲 (T_2) 便带我到旗台上去看星 (R_2)。(p47)

(60b) My mother (T_1) kept early hours (R_1), so, after she went indoors (T_2), my father would take me to the naval ship bridge to watch the stars (R_2). (p52)

In Example(60), the element "so, after she went indoors", which cannot be found in the source text, is added by the translator into the target text to act as the theme of the second clause.

2. The translator merges some clauses of the original text and makes both theme and rheme of a certain clause act as a new theme.

(61a) 一阵阵的青草香 (T_1)，从微风里荡过来 (R_1)，我们 (T_2) 慢步地走着，陡觉神气清爽，一尘不染 (R_2)。(p85)

(61b) The aroma of green grass carried over fitfully by the breeze (T) made us instantly feel refreshed (R). (p89)

In Example(61), both the theme "一阵阵的青草香" and the rheme "从微风里荡过来" of the first clause in the original Chinese text are merged into the nominal phrase "The aroma of green grass carried over fitfully by the breeze" to act as the theme of the clause in the target text.

3. The translator makes part of the theme of a clause serve as a new theme, with the rest of the original theme becoming part of the new rheme.

(62a) 同他们做朋友的 (T)，除了有时上山来的少数乡下人外，就是

几只猛虎 (R)。(p181)

(62b) They (T) had for company only a number of tigers apart from a few country folks who occasionally came up the mountain for a visit (R). (p183)

In Example(62), just one part of the theme "同他们做朋友的" of the original clause, that is, "They", is employed as the new theme of the target clause, with the rest of the original theme becoming part of the new rheme.

(63a) 可惜我 (T) 不能走到这座深山，去和猛虎为友 (R)。(p181)

(63b) It's a pity (T) that I'm unable to go to the mountain to make friends with the fierce tigers (R). (p183)

In Example(63), the original theme "可惜我" of the Chinese clause is split into two parts in the English version, with "It's a pity" as the theme and "I" as part of the rheme.

4. The translator leaves the original theme untranslated, just translates the original rheme of a clause into English, and makes part of the rheme to serve as a new theme.

(64a) 想到了这些实际 (T)，便觉得杜鹃这种鸟大可以作为欺世盗名者的标本了 (R)。(p80)

(64b) Hence I believe that the cuckoo (T) can best serve as a model of those who win popularity by dishonest means (R). (p82)

In Example(64), the original theme "想到了这些实际" of the Chinese clause remains untranslated, and part of the original rheme, that is, "Hence I believe that the cuckoo", becomes the new theme of the English clause.

5. The translator makes the original theme of a clause together with part of its rheme become a new theme.

(65a) 而且实际上说来，吹牛 (T) 对于一个人的确有极大的妙用 (R)。(p95)

(65b) That boasting is of extremely great use to one (T) is beyond doubt (R). (p97)

In Example(65), the theme of the English translated clause, "That boasting is of extremely great use to one", is made up of both the original theme "吹牛" and part of the original rheme "对于一个人有极大的妙用".

(66a) 经过三十年的长岁月 (T)，人应该忘记了许多事情 (R)。(p182)

(66b) Things that happened some thirty years ago (T) are apt to be forgotten (R). (p184)

In Example(66), the original theme "经过三十年的长岁月" and part of the original rheme "许多事情" in the Chinese clause work together to act as the theme of the English clause, namely, "Things that happened some thirty years ago".

6. The translator renders the original theme into one clause with its own theme and rheme by separating the original clause.

(67a) 一般人对于时间的悟性 (T_1)，似乎只够支配搭船、乘车的短时间 (R_1)；对于百年的长期间的寿命 (T_2)，他们不能胜任 (R_2)。(p153)

(67b) Ordinary people (T_1) have only a superficial understanding of time (R_1). They (T_2) seem to know it only as regards such small matters as boarding a train or boat, but not in things concerning a lifetime (R_2). (p158)

In Example(67), the original theme of the first Chinese clause "一般人对于时间的悟性" turns into one clause in its English version, with its own theme "Ordinary people" and rheme "have only a superficial understanding of time".

It should be pointed out that thematic transference generally falls into two categories. The first type is called obligatory thematic transference, which is caused by the distinct linguistic norms of the two languages. The other type is termed as selective thematic transference, which is due to a translator's preference for a certain style of expressing. Here is one instance of the obligatory thematic transference.

(68a) 我 (T_1) 愈怕 (R_1)，狗 (T_2) 愈凶 (R_2)。(p176)

(68b) And the more scared (T_1) I was (R_1), the fiercer (T_2) he became (R_2). (p177)

In Example(68), the thematic transference from "我" and "狗" in the original text to "And the more scared" and "the fiercer" respectively is caused by the different syntactic structures between Chinese and English.

Since English and Chinese belong to different language families and cultural systems, there are great systematic differences between the two languages. Therefore, the transference of TP patterns in textual translation will definitely be restricted at both linguistic and cultural levels. The differences in thinking modes between English and Chinese nations are the deep roots of the differences in syntactic structure and textual structure between English and Chinese languages. Certain textual patterns reflect certain thinking patterns, so the differences in patterns of thematic progression between English and Chinese languages also mirror the differences in textual construction as well as in thinking modes between English and Chinese nations.

After the transference of TP patterns in Chinese-English textual translation are investigated by observing, describing and analyzing the existing translated texts, it is found that in most cases patterns of TP in the original texts are changed by the translator, which is directly due to the change of Theme in the process of translating. However, the underlying constraints of these transference are as follows: first of all, Chinese is a topic-prominent, paratactic language whereas English is a subject-prominent, hypotactic language. Apart from that, different thinking patterns between the English and Chinese nations and the translator's purpose in his translating action both play a certain role in the translation. All these factors constrain the translator's choices in textual translation at the linguistic or cultural level, resulting in different kinds of changes in terms of TP patterns in the translation.

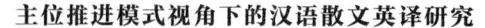

Chapter 7

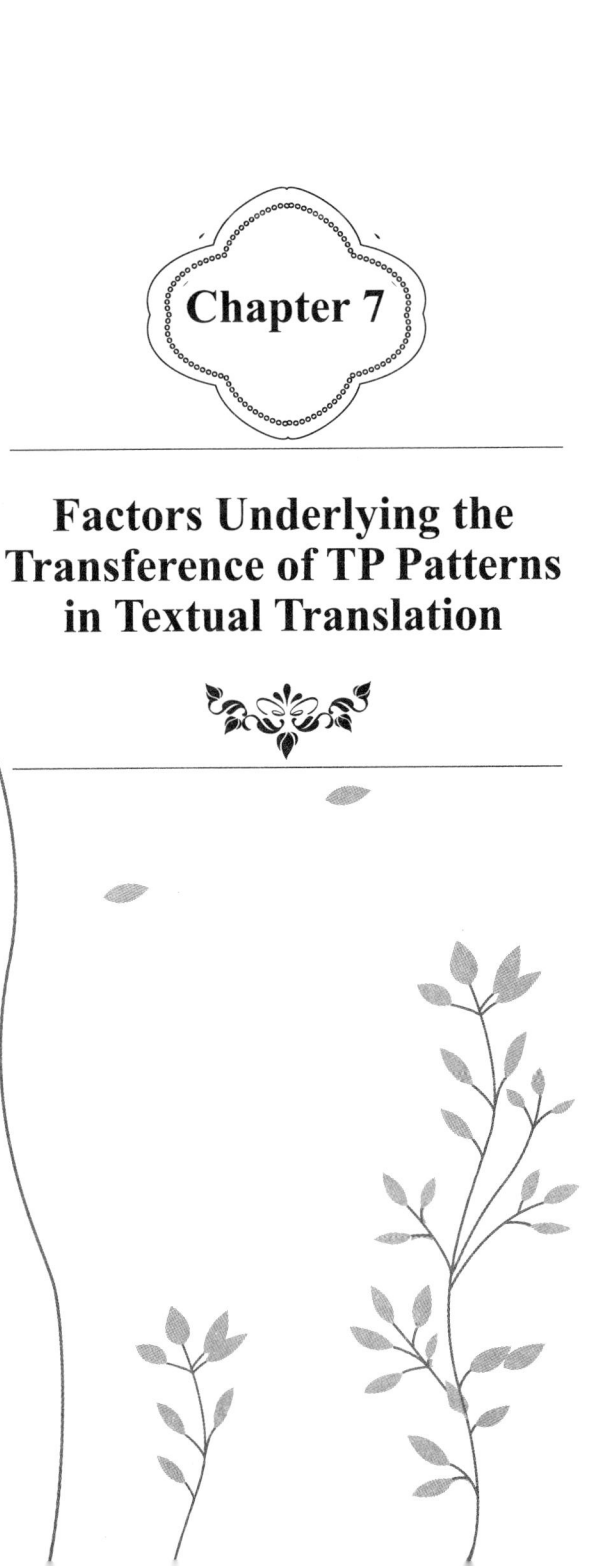

Factors Underlying the Transference of TP Patterns in Textual Translation

Thematic Progression is invented to study how Theme in a text is developed from clause to clause or to larger stretches of a text. TP plays an important role in maintaining coherence in a text and it is closely related to the method of development in the text. TP patterns are the forms of arranging the linguistic materials in a text, and they are the important means in fulfilling the textual functions, for they are of help not only to writers in producing their texts but also to translators in interpreting the source texts. TP patterns display the framework and overall orientation of a text and reflect the author's methods and rhetorical intentions of creating the text, so they serve as an important tool in textual translation. Great differences exist between Chinese and English due to the quite different linguistic and cultural systems they belong to, so the transference of TP patterns in Chinese-English textual translation are surely subject to the restrictions of various factors such as linguistic factors and cultural factors. Translator's idiosyncrasy also contributes to the transference of TP patterns. All these factors will be explored in this chapter in order to explain the underlying reasons for the different manners in transferring TP patterns.

7.1 Linguistic Factors

7.1.1 Subject-Prominent VS Topic-Prominent

According to the new linguistic typology advanced by American linguists Charles Li and Sandra Thompson (Li, 1976; Li & Thompson, 1981), English is a subject-prominent language whereas Chinese is a topic-prominent language. The themes of clauses in English are mostly overlapped with the subjects of the clauses. In English, "there tends to be a very high correlation between theme / rheme and subject / predicate in the Hallidayan model. The correlation does not hold in the case of marked themes, but, generally speaking, the distinction between theme and rheme is more or less identical to the traditional grammatical distinction between subject and predicate." (Baker, 2000:123) However, the clauses in Chinese are generally lacking such explicit formal features as displayed clearly in English clauses, and they are often organized into a text on the basis of their inner meanings. Those clauses with comments centering around a topic abound in Chinese. "A clause in Chinese is essentially a semantic structure typical of 'topic + comment', and the theme in a clause is virtually the topic of it." (Li, 2001:200) Moreover, one feature of topic in the Chinese language is that "once an element is announced as topic, this element may be omitted altogether in subsequent clauses, hence the proliferation of subjectless clauses …" (Baker, 2000:142)

Therefore, in conducting textual translation between English and Chinese, at the clause level, a translator has to handle properly the issue of thematic

Chapter 7 Factors Underlying the Transference of TP Patterns in Textual Translation

transference between the two languages, which is, to a considerable degree, tantamount to dealing with tactfully the transference between "subject + predicate" structure in English clauses and "topic + comment" structure in Chinese clauses. In English-Chinese translation, the issue of thematic transference is mainly about how to transfer subject in English to topic in Chinese by means of re-arranging those themes, and in Chinese-English translation, the issue of thematic transference is largely concerned with how to make use of "subject + predicate" pattern in English to take the place of "topic + comment" pattern in Chinese.

At the text level, when a topic appears in a Chinese text or paragraph, then various relevant information can be organized and developed around this topic. More often than not, a piece of Chinese text is unfolded around a certain topic, and sometimes the connections between themes and rhemes of the clauses in the text are not obvious and the textual structure seems rather loose, but the whole text still maintains semantic coherence. In an English text or paragraph, the information is usually organized through theme and gradually moves forward. This is the difference in organizing information at the text level between Chinese and English. In such cases, if a translator merely duplicates the TP patterns found in the original text when translating from Chinese to English and loads the themes of clauses in the target text with diverse information, he is likely to produce a translated text with loose textual structure and chaotic flow of information. So, under such conditions, a translator normally needs to adjust the TP patterns of the source text so as to create a well-arranged textual layout and orderly information flow in the target text.

As the statistical results indicate, this difference in linguistic features between Chinese and English is mainly reflected in the mutual transference between TP with a constant theme and linear TP, as well as in the transference from crisscrossed TP to TP with a constant theme in Chinese-English textual translation. Of all the causes responsible for the changes of TP patterns in the translating process, topic theme in Chinese being transferred to subject theme in English is an important one, which is directly caused by the subject-prominent feature of the English language and the topic-prominent feature of the Chinese language.

7.1.2 Hypotaxis VS Parataxis

"'Hypotaxis' refers to linking words or clauses by means of formal devices (both lexical and morphological) possessed by a language whereas 'parataxis' refers to linking words or clauses through their inner meanings or logical connections instead of formal devices in a language. The former places stress on formal cohesion of the clauses while the latter puts emphasis on semantic coherence of the whole text." (Liu, 1992:18-19) The English language attaches importance to hypotaxis and in the construction of clauses and texts it "often resorts to various formal devices to arrange words, clauses or sentences, and focuses on overt cohesion, completeness of syntactic structure as well as expressing meaning through form." (Lian, 1993:48) In contrast, the Chinese language gives priority to parataxis and in the construction of clauses and texts it "seldom or never makes use of formal cohesive devices, and focuses on covert coherence, logical sequence of things, linguistic functions and meanings, as well as using meaning to govern form." (ibid:53) As two different ways of expressing ideas in languages, the differences between hypotaxis and parataxis are reflected not only in syntactic structure but also in textual structure.

Chapter 7 Factors Underlying the Transference of TP Patterns in Textual Translation

The differences in textual structure between English and Chinese, caused by their distinct characteristics of expression, namely, hypotaxis versus parataxis, are also embodied in the patterns of cohesion and progression of themes and rhemes in a piece of text. In English texts, textual cohesion and coherence are highly achieved through the orderly progression of themes and rhemes of the clauses. The connections of these themes and rhemes are realized by the formal resources in English such as grammatical and lexical devices to show their relations and to maintain semantic coherence, and then to express the meaning and logical relations of the whole text. To sum up, English texts attach great importance to overt cohesion, complete layout of text, and the use of more formal connectives to express meaning.

However, in Chinese texts, the connections and progression of themes and rhemes are sometimes not obvious, and the cohesion of themes and rhemes of neighbouring clauses is less maintained by formal cohesive devices, and the logical relations in the whole text are mainly expressed through semantic integration of various clauses. In brief, the Chinese texts give prominence to covert coherence and put form under the governance of meaning.

The differences in hypotaxis versus parataxis between English and Chinese exert great influences on the TP patterns employed in the construction of texts. As far as TP with a constant theme is concerned, English texts often resort to the reference function of pronouns and the use of the definite article to show the cohesion of themes of different clauses whereas Chinese texts usually lay stress on semantic coherence and avoid the repetition of pronouns. Generally speaking, after the theme of the first clause appears, then it is omitted in the subsequent clauses, thus TP with zero theme emerges.

This explains why the statistical results indicate that TP with zero theme occurs much frequently in the original Chinese texts while there is only one instance of such pattern, which comes under the influence of the original pattern of the source text, in the English translated texts. This is the impact on textual translation between Chinese and English brought about by the respective hypotactic and paratactic characteristics of these two languages. Therefore, in Chinese-English textual translation, a translator normally transfers TP with zero theme in Chinese texts to TP with a constant theme in English texts, which is indeed the most notable law of transference of TP patterns with the highest frequency of occurrences in the statistical results. Apart from that, TP with zero theme in the original Chinese texts is occasionally transferred by the translator to linear TP in the translated texts so as to produce an English version with both orderly thematic connections and clear logical relations.

7.2 Different Thinking Patterns Between Chinese and English

Different thinking patterns exist between different peoples and cultures. The process of constructing texts is actually the projections of the thinking process in the form of language, so the differences in thinking patterns determine the differences in textual structures. The Chinese people have different traits in thinking patterns from the English-speaking nations, so the Chinese language displays different syntactic structures and textual layouts from the English language, and they will differ in the choice of TP patterns in the construction of texts.

The differences in thinking patterns between the Chinese nation and English-speaking nations are reflected in the following aspects. Firstly, "the

Chinese people emphasize overall thought and integral formula, presented as synthetic thinking pattern. Westerners, however, stress individual thought and structural formula, presented as analytic thinking mode." (Zhang et al., 1996:9) Therefore, the synthetic thinking pattern is reflected in the Chinese language as the preference for an overall framework, the proliferation of topic-prominent clauses, and the arranging of clauses around a certain topic in accordance with logical sequence, so the Chinese texts are usually loose in structure but compact in meaning. The analytic thinking pattern is presented in the English language as the stress on well-arranged structure and precise logic, and the profusion of subject-predicate clauses. Normally, the subject of an English clause cannot be omitted and the other components cannot be casually chosen and arranged.

Secondly, "Western aesthetics attaches much importance to logical thinking and rational cognition, and at the same time places stress on the formal demonstration, thus it forms an inclination for rational thinking. By contrast, the traditional Chinese aesthetics gives priority to perceptual thinking and knowledge from experience, so it forms a mindset of thinking which emphasizes stream of thought but ignores the logical demonstration." (Zhang et al., 1996:11) As a result, under the impact of these two different thinking patterns, namely, Westerners stress logical thinking while the Chinese nation emphasizes fuzzy thinking, the English language exhibits different characteristics from the Chinese language, namely, English is hypotaxis-based, with compact linguistic forms and overt grammar while Chinese is parataxis-based, with diffusive linguistic forms and covert grammar. "The fuzzy thinking mode of the Chinese nation causes the Chinese language to be flexible and concise in the use of logical connectives, thus definitely making the language assume paratactic features. The formal and logical thinking pattern of the English-speaking nations causes the English language to rely on various connectives in expressing logical relations, thus inevitably makes the language take on hypotactic features." (Zhang et al., 2001:17)

Apart from that, some other differences between the Chinese nation and English-speaking nations in thinking patterns are as follows: "the thinking patterns of English-speaking nations are abstract, linear, antithetic, and subject-centered, whereas the thinking patterns of the Chinese nation are concrete, curvilinear, unified, thus integrating subject with object in language use." (Wang, 2001:82)

The different thinking patterns between the Chinese nation and English-speaking nations are reflected not only in the clause level but also in the text level. The English texts mainly make use of formal devices to express various kinds of meaning and logical relations, and mostly resort to grammatical and lexical resources to link different clauses and to organize texts. In an English paragraph, formal devices are often employed to arrange semantic contents and every clause in the paragraph are closely connected with the main topic of the paragraph so that the meaning of the paragraph can be expressed in a clear and methodical way. An English paragraph is clause-based, usually composed of a series of complete clauses, and each clause is developed or split from the preceding clause, so the development of an English paragraph often exhibits linear feature. In making sentences and constructing texts, the English language lays emphasis on the formal cohesion, which works together with various morphological devices to create well-formed clauses as well as well-arranged texts.

However, the Chinese texts are not so much form-restricted as English texts in textual structure. Few or no such formal cohesive devices are required to build Chinese texts. Instead, they are normally constructed by means of semantic devices, inner logical connections and context. So the textual structure seems quite covert and sometimes loose, but clear in inner logic and meaning. In arranging different clauses to produce a text, the Chinese language focuses on the inner meanings and logical sequence of things, and merely resorts to the logical connections between meanings of words and clauses, without the help of formal devices, to construct a coherent text. This also mirrors such characteristics of the language as emphasis on the overall framework of text and the governing function of meaning over form. The Chinese texts can be seen to a large extent as a stream of meanings which are organized into a whole on the basis of parataxis. The proliferation of streamlined clauses as well as somewhat haphazard division of paragraphs characterizes the Chinese texts.

Due to the writing styles and consequent textual features caused by the thinking patterns of the Chinese people, TP with no regular pattern abounds in the original Chinese texts, which can be seen clearly from the statistical results. This pattern is mostly transferred to linear TP and sometimes changed into one clause in the English versions because the translator frequently resorts to formal devices of the English language in organizing texts and expressing meanings in order to cater to the textual norms of the English language, which are constrained by the thinking patterns of the English nation. Of all the causes responsible for the changes of TP patterns, both topic theme in Chinese being transferred to subject theme in English and implicit theme in Chinese being transferred to explicit theme in English are actually influenced by the different characteristics of the two languages, which are constrained at the deep level by the different thinking patterns of the two peoples.

On one hand, the differences in thinking patterns between these two peoples basically restrict the characteristics of these two languages and influence their evolution and development, and they serve as the deep-seated fountainhead of the differences in syntactic structure and textual layout between Chinese and English. On the other hand, a certain textual pattern mirrors a specific thinking pattern, so the differences in TP patterns between Chinese and English are the projections of different thinking patterns between the Chinese nation and English-speaking nations onto the field of textual construction.

7.3 Translator's Purposes

Undoubtedly, linguistic and cultural differences exist between two different languages, but how these differences affect textual translation is ultimately determined by the translator. As one form of communication across cultures, translating is a purposeful activity performed by a translator and it is defined as "a complex action designed to achieve a particular purpose." (Nord, 2001:13) The basic idea of *Skopos* theory proposed by German Functionalist school of translation studies is that "the top-ranking rule for any translation is thus the '*Skopos* rule', which says that a translational action is determined by its *Skopos*." (ibid:29) A translator always partakes of some specific purpose when he is engaged in a translating activity, so the intended functions of the translated texts determine the strategies and methods adopted by the translator in the translating process, and the translator's choice of specific translation strategies and methods determine, to a large degree, textual structure of the translated texts as well as the transference of TP patterns between original texts and target texts.

In the preface of the book from which we select materials, the translator tells the readers that "a panoramic view of modern Chinese prose writings will strike us with their abundance and variety, and among them there is no lack of excellent pieces of writing which deserve recommendation to the outside world."(Zhang, 2003: preface) His purpose in translating these prose writings into English is "to present brilliant Chinese culture to the world" and "to offer a window through which foreign scholars can understand and study the evolution of ideas of Chinese intelligentsia since May 4th Movement of 1919" (Zhang, 2003: preface). Since the translator translates with the intention of helping those foreign readers who has little or no knowledge of the Chinese language to obtain an understanding of contents and ideas contained in the original prose writings, so he will try his best to make his translations function in the target context in such a way as the target audience expect, that is to say, to transmit effectively the message contained in the source texts and meanwhile to cater for the aesthetic expectations of the target readers so that his translated texts can be easily followed and accepted by them.

The prospective readers are the target for whom a translator produces translations. Therefore, in order to fulfill the desired purposes and functions of the translated texts, the translator will definitely show great concern over the cultural background, reader's expectations and reception ability of the target audience, and then work out corresponding translation strategies and methods. Nida (2001:95) points out that "the greater the differences in the source and target cultures, the greater the need for adjustments ... The greater the differences in social and educational levels of the source and target audiences, the greater the number of adjustments." As far as our selected materials are concerned, all the source texts are prose writings produced from 1920s to 1940s by modern Chinese writers. Due to the differences in cultural background, thinking mode and linguistic norms, there is a big gap between the intentions of the authors as well as the textual structures they employed and the reception ability of the target audience, because the prospective readers from English-speaking countries generally lack the background knowledge of Chinese society, history and culture, which forces the translator to make proper adjustments so as to bridge the gap.

Consequently, the translator proceeds from his considerations of the target audience in the process of translating and chooses translation strategies in line with the intended readers and expected functions of his translations. On one hand, he will consider carefully how to effectively transmit the information and ideas contained in these prose texts in order to fulfill his translation purpose, thus he gives priority to the semantic contents but little regard to the formal traits of the source texts. On the other hand, he must take great pains to construct the translated texts in accordance with the linguistic and textual norms of English so as to ensure the readability and acceptability of his translations in a new environment.

As a result, the translator mainly refers to the textual norms of English in constructing the target texts, which leads to the low ratio of keeping the original TP patterns of the source texts in all the transference. As is shown by the statistical results, this is most noticeable in the transference from TP with a constant theme to one clause, from TP with zero theme to one clause and from linear TP to one clause just because the translator often re-organize clauses in the original texts in order to make textual structure clear in the translated texts. However, the translator will inevitably receive influences of the source texts, hence the cases of those unchanged TP patterns in translation. This can be seen clearly in the 154 cases of unchanged TP patterns shown in Table 5. It goes without saying that any translation will bear the imprint of a translator's style, so it is natural for the translator to conduct linguistic transference with personal preference in the process of translating, which will, to some degree, produce an impact on the textual structure of translated texts and the transference of TP patterns. In some cases the mutual transference between TP with a constant theme and linear TP can be better explained for this reason.

Chapter 8

Suggestions for Future Research

8.1 Findings of the Present Research

After the descriptions and statistical analysis of our selected materials, the following findings are made.

Firstly, in the existing translated texts, the ratio of keeping the TP patterns of the source texts is low in Chinese-English textual translation, which is caused by the linguistic and cultural differences between Chinese and English, as well as translation strategies and methods adopted by the translator.

Secondly, there are ten types of transference of TP patterns with high frequency of occurrence among all the transference, which represent, to a considerable extent, the laws of transference of TP patterns in Chinese-English textual translation.

Thirdly, conducting observations on the basis of paragraph, it is discovered that there is correlation between the transference of TP patterns and the length of a paragraph. Generally speaking, the shorter a paragraph is, the greater the possibility of maintaining the original TP patterns is; the longer a paragraph, particularly when the paragraph contains several sentence groups, the greater the probability that a translator tends to adjust even reconstruct TP patterns in his translating process.

Fourthly, the change of TP patterns is generally caused by the change of themes and rhemes at the clause level. Sometimes several occurrences of thematic changes work together to bring about one occurrence of change of TP pattern. So the statistical results indicate that the occurrences of thematic changes are more than the occurrences of changes of TP patterns. There are, of course, some cases in which the theme changes but the TP pattern does not.

Fifthly, as far as the transference of TP patterns is concerned, the translated texts show a tendency of normalization, which is reflected in the frequent use of the two commonest TP patterns, namely, TP with a constant theme and linear TP, as well as in the low frequency of occurrences of some other TP patterns.

8.2 Limitations of the Present Research

The above-mentioned conclusions still need to be tested by further study because the present research has some limitations. Firstly, the sample selected for our research is small in scale, which will affect to a certain degree the validity of the research results as well as the universal applicability of the research conclusions. Secondly, all the selected materials used for this research are the translated texts produced by one translator, which will make the research conclusions subject to the influence of the translator's style.

8.3 Suggestions for Further Research

In view of the limitations of the present study mentioned above, further research should be conducted in the following respects in order to gain a better understanding of the issue. Firstly, in-depth studies based on large-scale data still need to be carried out in order to probe into the universal laws of transference of TP patterns in text-oriented translation. Secondly, the materials selected for future study should contain translated texts produced by various translators, which will enable us to investigate the strategies and methods adopted in transferring TP patterns from the perspective of translators. Thirdly, multilingual translated texts can be incorporated into the selected materials to ensure the universal applicability of the research conclusions.

References

[1] AUSTEN J. Sense and Sensitivity [M]. Beijing: World Publishing Corporation, 2007.

[2] BAKER M. In Other Words: A Coursebook on Translation[M]. Beijing: Foreign Language Teaching and Research Press, 2000.

[3] BAKER M . Routledge Encyclopedia of Translation Studies[M]. Shanghai: Shanghai Foreign Language Education Press, 2004.

[4] DANES F. Functional sentence perspective and the organization of the text[M]. The Hague: Mouton, 1974.

[5] FAWCETT P. Translation and Language: Linguistic Theories Explained[M]. Beijing: Foreign Language Teaching and Research Press, 2007.

[6] GHADESSY M, Gao Y. Small corpora and translation: Comparing thematic organization in two languages[M]. Amsterdam: John Benjamins, 2001.

[7] HALLIDAY M A K. An Introduction to Functional Grammar[M]. Beijing: Foreign Language Teaching and Research Press, 2000.

[8] HATIM B. Text linguistics and translation[M]. Shanghai: Shanghai Foreign Language Education Press, 2004.

[9] HATIM B. Communication Across Cultures: Translation Theory and Contrastive Text Linguistics[M]. Shanghai: Shanghai Foreign Language Education Press, 2001.

[10] HATIM B, I MASON. Discourse and the Translator[M]. Shanghai: Shanghai Foreign Language Education Press, 2001.

[11] HOLMES J. The Name and Nature of Translation Studies[M]. Amsterdam: Rodopi, 1988.

[12] HUANG G W. Experiential Enhanced Theme in English[M]. Norwood, New Jersey: Ablex Publishing Corporation, 1996.

[13] LI C N. Subject and topic: a new typology of language[M]. London: Academic Press, 1976.

[14] LI C N, S A Thompson. Mandarin Chinese: A Functional Reference Grammar[M]. Berkeley: University of California Press, 1981.

[15] MARTIN J R. English Text: System and Structure [M]. Amsterdam: John Benjamins, 1992.

[16] NIDA E A. Language and Culture: Contexts in Translating[M]. Shanghai: Shanghai Foreign Language Education Press, 2001.

[17] NIDA E A, C R Taber. The Theory and Practice of Translation [M]. Shanghai: Shanghai Foreign Language Education Press, 2004.

[18] NORD C. Translating as a Purposeful Activity: Functionalist Approaches Explained[M]. Shanghai: Shanghai Foreign Language Education Press, 2001.

[19] PAPEGAAIJ B, K Schubert. Text Coherence in Translation[M]. Dordrecht: Foris, 1988.

[20] THOMPSON G. Introducing Functional Grammar[M]. Beijing: Foreign Language Teaching and Research Press, 2000.

[21] TOURY G. Descriptive Translation Studies and Beyond[M]. Shanghai: Shanghai Foreign Language Education Press, 2001.

[22] VENTOLA E. Thematic development and translation[M]. London: Pinter, 1995.

[23] 曹进, 李苑莞. 网络新闻语篇中的主位与主位推进模式特征研究 [J]. 天津外国语大学学报, 2021(3): 106–116.

[24] 曹志宏, 李玲. Nature 中论文摘要的主位推进模式分析 [J]. 西安电子科技大学学报（社会科学版）, 2015(6): 104–111.

[25] 成丽芳. 超句意识、主位结构与汉译英主语的确定 [J]. 中国科技翻译, 2006 (2): 16–18.

[26] 董敏. 从主位推进分析看司法判决推理 [J]. 北京理工大学学报（社会科学版）, 2010(3): 123-127.

[27] 方开瑞. 翻译描写研究与翻译学建设 [J]. 山东外语教学, 2001 (2): 23-26.

[28] 方丽. 主位推进程序与中国学生的英语语篇思维模式 [J]. 四川外语学院学报, 2004(2): 76-79.

[29] 方琰, 艾晓霞. 汉语语篇主位进程结构分析 [J]. 外语研究, 1995 (2): 20-24.

[30] 高健. 英文散文一百篇 [M]. 北京：中国对外翻译出版公司, 2001.

[31] 国防. 信息性英文摘要主位推进规律及主位结构特征的研究 [J]. 国外外语教学, 2007(3): 41-46.

[32] 胡壮麟. 语篇的衔接与连贯 [M]. 上海：上海外语教育出版社, 1994.

[33] 黄国文. 语篇分析概要 [M]. 长沙：湖南教育出版社, 1988.

[34] 黄国文. 英语强势主位结构的句法 — 语义分析 [J]. 外语教学与研究, 1996 (3): 44-48.

[35] 黄萍, 胡力方. 基于体裁理论的中文仲裁书引言主位推进模式分析 [J]. 外国语文, 2014(1): 79-82.

[36] 黄衍. 试论英语主位和述位 [J]. 外国语, 1985 (5): 32-36.

[37] 姜望琪. 主位概念的嬗变 [J]. 当代语言学, 2008 (2): 137-146.

[38] 李国庆. 主位推进模式与语篇体裁：《老人与海》分析 [J]. 外语与外语教学, 2003(7): 53-56.

[39] 李健, 范祥涛. 基于主位推进模式的语篇翻译研究 [J]. 语言与翻译, 2008(1): 62-66.

[40] 李诗芳. 论主位推进模式与英汉语篇模式间的关系——基于语篇翻译的视角 [J]. 黑龙江高教研究, 2009(8): 193-194.

[41] 李运兴. 语篇翻译引论 [M]. 北京：中国对外翻译出版公司, 2001.

[42] 李运兴. "主位"概念在翻译研究中的应用 [J]. 外语与外语教学, 2002 (7): 19-22.

[43] 李战子. 主位推进和篇章连贯性 [J]. 外语教学, 1992 (1): 1-6.

[44] 连淑能. 英汉对比研究 [M]. 北京：高等教育出版社, 1993.

[45] 刘爱军. 基于语料库的译者风格比较研究——以朱自清散文英译为例 [J]. 外语电化教学, 2020 (4): 101–105.

[46] 刘富丽. 英汉翻译中的主位推进模式 [J]. 外语教学与研究, 2006 (5): 309–312.

[47] 刘礼进, 郭慧君, 彭保良. 英汉广播新闻话语中的主位选择和主位推进 [J]. 外语学刊, 2014(5): 61–68.

[48] 刘宓庆. 汉英对比与翻译 [M]. 南昌: 江西教育出版社, 1992.

[49] 刘士聪, 余东. 试论以主/述位作翻译单位 [J]. 外国语, 2000 (3): 61–66.

[50] 吕岩. 主位推进模式及其在英语写作教学中的应用 [J]. 四川外语学院学报, 2009(2): 60–62.

[51] 马静. 主位推进、语义衔接与英语写作的连贯性——四、六级范型作文分析 [J]. 外语教学, 2001(5): 45–50.

[52] 苗兴伟. 英语的评价型强势主位结构 [J]. 山东外语教学, 2007 (2): 54–57.

[53] 彭发胜. 主语驱动原则下的汉语散文英译策略研究 [J]. 外语教学与研究, 2016 (1): 128–138.

[54] 乔萍, 翟淑蓉, 宋洪玮. 散文佳作108篇 [M]. 南京: 译林出版社, 2002.

[55] 史金生, 娜仁图雅, 宋轩. 规定性语体的主位推进研究——兼谈主位推进模式与篇章类型及主题的关系 [J]. 语言文字应用, 2018(1): 90–99.

[56] 孙万彪, 王恩铭. 高级翻译教程（第四版）[M]. 上海: 上海外语教育出版社, 2011.

[57] 唐耀彩. 散文翻译中的跨句法——兼评张培基《英译中国现代散文选》[J]. 北京第二外国语学院学报, 2001 (4): 57–62, 86.

[58] 王斌. 主位推进的翻译解构与结构功能 [J]. 中国翻译, 2000 (1): 35–37.

[59] 王桂珍. 主题、主位与汉语句子主题的英译 [J]. 现代外语, 1996 (4): 46–50.

[60] 王洪涛. 从"含蓄朦胧"到"显豁明晰"——以中西比较美学为指归的散文英译研究 [J]. 外语教学, 2006 (1): 61–64.

[61] 王俊华. 主位、主语和话题——论三者在英汉翻译中的关系及其相互转换 [J]. 西安外国语学院学报, 2006 (1): 24–27.

[62] 王琦, 程晓堂. 语篇中的主位推进与信息参数 [J]. 外语学刊, 2004 (2): 48–52.

[63] 王扬. 思维模式差异及其对语篇的影响 [J]. 四川外语学院学报, 2001 (1): 81–83.

[64] 王寅. 主位、主语和话题的思辨——兼谈英汉核心句型 [J]. 外语研究, 1999 (3): 15–19.

[65] 项名健. 英语科技语篇中的主位推进模式链定量分析 [J]. 西北农林科技大学学报（社会科学版）, 2008(6): 136–140.

[66] 徐盛桓. 主位和述位 [J]. 外语教学与研究, 1982 (1): 1–9.

[67] 杨斐翡. 主位推进与语篇连贯 [J]. 西安外国语学院学报, 2004 (4): 7–10.

[68] 杨萌. 英语语篇连贯衔接性分析——主位推进与衔接纽带 [J]. 西北大学学报（哲学社会科学版）, 2012(3): 189–191.

[69] 杨明. 英译汉中的主位与话题 [J]. 外语学刊, 2003 (3): 84–88.

[70] 杨明. 汉译英中的主题、主语与主位 [J]. 山东外语教学, 2006 (3): 23–28.

[71] 杨信彰. 从主位看英汉翻译中的意义等值问题 [J]. 解放军外国语学院学报, 1996 (1): 44–48.

[72] Yang, Yulan. [杨玉兰]. 论散文翻译中审美效果的艺术再现–以《荷塘月色》的英译为例. 四川外语学院学报, 2008 (6): 102-104.

[73] 张德禄, 刘洪民. 主位结构与语篇连贯 [J]. 外语研究, 1994 (3): 27–33.

[74] 张道振. 主位推进与译文连贯的意谓 [J]. 天津外国语学院学报, 2006 (5): 22–27.

[75] 张克定. 英语存在句强势主位的语义语用分析 [J]. 解放军外国语学院学报, 1998 (2): 39–45.

[76] 张曼. 意识流小说中主位推进模式的变异与连贯 [J]. 西安外国语学院学报, 2005(4): 1–3.

[77] 张培基. 英译中国现代散文选（第 2 辑）[M]. 上海：上海外语教育出版社, 2003.

[78] 张思洁, 张柏然. 试从中西思维模式的差异论英汉两种语言的特点 [J]. 解放军外国语学院学报, 1996 (5): 8–12.

[79] 张思洁, 张柏然. 形合与意合的哲学思维反思 [J]. 中国翻译, 2001 (4): 13-18.

[80] 张育红. 主位推进与写作的连贯性 [J]. 国外外语教学, 2004(2): 47-50.

[81] 赵小品, 胡梅红. 主位推进与衔接手段在汉译英中的应用 [J]. 山东外语教学, 2003 (3): 76-80.

[82] 郑贵友. 汉语句子实义切分的宏观原则与主位的确定 [J]. 语言教学与研究, 2000 (4): 18-24.

[83] 钟茂生, 王小虎. 汉语篇章主位推进模式自动识别方法 [J]. 计算机应用研究, 2015(5): 1313–1315,1329.

[84] 朱曼华. 中国散文翻译的新收获——喜读张培基教授《英译中国现代散文选》[J]. 中国翻译, 2000 (3): 61–63.

[85] 朱永生. 主位推进模式与语篇分析 [J]. 外语教学与研究, 1995 (3): 6–12.

[86] 朱永生, 严世清. 系统功能语言学多维思考 [M]. 上海: 上海外语教育出版社, 2001.

Appendix

The following abbreviations are used in the book.

CP	Compound Pattern
CTP	crisscrossed TP
DTS	Descriptive Translation Studies
ETC	Enhanced Theme Construction
FTP	framework TP
ITP	intermittent TP
LTP	linear TP
OC	One Clause
PTP	parallel TP
R	Rheme
ST	Source Text
T	Theme
TL	Target Language
TP	Thematic Progression
TPAT	TP with two alternate themes
TPCR	TP with a continuous rheme
TPCT	TP with a constant theme
TPDT	TP with derived themes
TPIE	TP with inserted elements

TPRP	TP with no regular pattern
TPSR	TP with a split rheme
TPTR	TP with merged theme(s) and rheme(s)
TPZT	TP with zero theme
TT	Target Text